I0749577

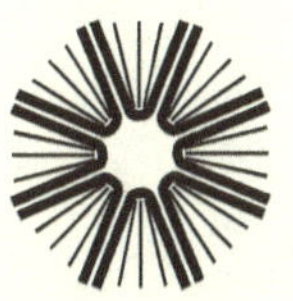

THE MUD OF A CENTURY

The Mud of a Century

Yūka Ishii

translated from the Japanese by Haydn Trowell

GAZEBO BOOKS – SUMMER HILL 2023

Gazebo Books
PO Box 375
Summer Hill
New South Wales 2130
Australia
gazebobooks.com.au

Originally written in Japanese as *Hyakunendoro*

First published in English translation by Gazebo Books, 2023

Original Japanese edition published by Shinchosha Publishing Co., Ltd., Tokyo. English language translation rights arranged with Shinchosha Publishing Co., Ltd. through The English Agency (Japan) Ltd.

National Library of Australia
Cataloguing-in-Publication Entry
Author: Yūka Ishii
The Mud of a Century
ISBN 978 0 6489011 9 8 (paperback)

Cover and interior design by Mountains Brown Press.
Cover and frontispiece image: Damon Kowarsky, *Udaipur VII*, etching and aquatint on paper. Courtesy of the artist.

Perhaps you could call it a stroke of karmic good fortune that I was able to experience a once-in-a-century flood only three and a half months after moving to Chennai.

It had been raining nonstop the day before, a torrential downpour. Classes were called off early in the afternoon and the students urged to return home. When I opened my windows the following morning I found my apartment building surrounded on all sides by a coffee-coloured river.

At that moment, my mobile rang. It was Ananda, one of my students.

'Today's lesson is cancelled because of the flood,' I said in measured, simple Japanese as I stared out over the brown water.

I managed to make out a voice on the other end of the line fading in and out. 'Yes… Sensei… Yes.'

Ananda was my point of contact for the class, helping to convey messages to the other students, and he was kind enough to call me this day as well.

I hung up and glanced at the front door of the house across the street. Judging by how the upper part of the gate emerged suddenly from the murky surface, the water level must have reached more than a metre in height. I would have to thank the gods and buddhas that my apartment was on the fifth floor of the building.

Yesterday, when I first noticed the intensity of the rain roaring outside the classroom window, I raised my face from the textbook and said, 'There might be a flood tomorrow.' It already felt like so much time had passed since, with a laugh, I wrote the Japanese word for *flood* – *kōzui* – on the whiteboard.

Through the window, I could see the faces of a family of five on the second floor of a house isolated amid the reddish-brown water. Further along to the right, a man and woman, probably a couple, both carrying large bags on their heads, were wading through muddy water reaching all the way up to their chests.

Keeping an eye on what was happening outside, I switched on my laptop and brought up the digital news feed of a local TV station.

The headline jumped out at me: *Once-in-a-Century Flood Strikes Chennai! The Adyar Bursts its Banks, Threatening all Districts of the City!*

As I read the article, I realised that I had forgotten to give the students a task to do at home during this down time. I snatched up my mobile to redial Ananda, but the only response was a voice on loop repeating the phrase *No connection.* I turned back to my computer, but the screen was occupied now by a *This page cannot be displayed* error message. In the end, all means of communication, including phone and internet access, had failed, just like the supply of running water and electricity the night before.

With Chennai being situated on the thermal equator, the weather tends to remain hot and humid all year round, with the warmest period being May through June. I arrived in the city in late August, so even though I had been able to avoid a direct encounter with the hottest part of the year, I was here right when the rainy season struck. Starting with a blast of terrible thunder that erupted in the early hours one morning, a heavy rain crashed down day after day throughout October and November, a relentless downpour that stretched through morning, noon, and evening. With the roads submerged, unnavigable by bus or motorbike, there were days when only two or three students might be able to reach the classroom. And then there were the power outages, stretching out for hours on end. Having only recently arrived in India for the first time in my life, I had half wondered whether this might not be the usual state of affairs here. But then last night the embankments of the Adyar River broke.

The company where I worked was located on the other side of the Adyar, only a fifteen-minute journey from my apartment on foot. My job was to cross the bridge every day to make my way to the office and teach Japanese to the employees there.

Before coming to India, I had found myself saddled with more debt than I could ever possibly hope to manage.

'I'll pay you back right away,' the man had promised

me. He was a self-proclaimed freelance writer, and I had been dating him for about six months. Most of his business, it seemed, came from contributing miscellaneous articles related in one way or another to horse races, but as I had no interest in that kind of thing, I hadn't actually read any of his work. He was the typical image of a freelancer, with a stubbly face, long hair that he always wore tied up in a ponytail, and a habit of using phrases like *just so you know* and *definitely*. 'I've already borrowed too much. I've been blacklisted by the Japan Credit Information Reference Centre, and I can't get anything more out of the credit companies. Just so you know, I'm going to get paid for that other job soon, so I'll definitely get it back to you by the end of the month. Definitely.'

I had no money of my own to lend him, and so seeing no other option, I ended up borrowing from a certain loan shark. Two days after handing him the money, I found that I could no longer get into contact with him. I still don't know if he ever received the payment for that *other job* that he was expecting to receive a month later. Before the week was out, enthusiastic debt collectors rolling their *R*s like gangsters began to call on me at home. Taken aback by the sheer number of those visits, I made some enquiries with the lenders, only to discover that the man had borrowed from more than a dozen companies using my name and a copy of my National Health Insurance card. Those debt collectors, representing moneylenders that performed no identity checks and refused no applicants, were all especially ardent about collecting their dues. They weren't in the habit of listening to explanations or excuses.

I was in trouble, and so pocketing my pride, I decided to ask my ex-husband, from whom I had separated a year earlier, for another loan. Truth be told, I had already borrowed from him before, more than once for that matter, and I still hadn't paid him back so much as a single yen. This would be the fifth time.

My ex-husband was a broker for a number of real estate and stock trading companies, an organiser of senior matchmaking parties, a mediator for what was euphemistically known as *compensated dating*, and a recruiter of seasonal staff for a deep-ocean fishing company. He had an office on the third floor of an elevator-less multi-tenant building in front of Takadanobaba Station in Tokyo. I asked for him at the reception desk, a simple affair which existed merely for appearance's sake. Thirty minutes later he came out to see me.

'I've found work for you,' he announced abruptly. 'In Chennai.'

'I've never been to Thailand…' I demurred, waving a hand in front of my face.

'Not *Chiang Mai*. *Chennai*. In southern India.'

'What kind of job?'

'As a Japanese teacher. There's an IT company there that deals with a lot of Japanese businesses. They're looking for someone to teach their staff the language.'

I didn't have any experience in Japanese language education, but seeing as I hadn't done anything at all to even begin to repay my ex-husband what I owed him, I didn't have the courage to refuse. The work would be done on an annual contract, and although the monthly salary seemed quite low in yen, the local living expenses were an order of magnitude cheaper than in Japan, so I should have some money left over at the end of each month – or so he explained.

'Make sure you send an international remittance to our account here every month. Right, you should have it all paid off in around five years, I think…'

'You know, I never mentioned this before, but I was actually brought up in the snow country…'

'Ah, but it costs a fair bit to convert Indian rupees to Japanese yen, so five years won't actually cut it. It could be seven or eight in total, maybe?'

Two days later, I went to the Tokyo branch of a company called Hindu Technologies and had an interview with the vice president, who, as it happened, was visiting on a business trip from Chennai. Then, for some unfathomable reason, I was offered the job right there on the spot. The complicated process of applying for an Indian working visa proceeded at a miraculous pace, and two weeks later, I found myself touching down in Chennai, with my first class scheduled for the very next day.

The first thing that I noticed upon somehow finding myself in this foreign city was how many people were dressed like the superhero Moonlight Mask. When I looked carefully, I realised that they were all women driving around on scooters, wearing sunglasses with scarves wrapped around their lower faces not to defend world peace, but to protect the health of their lungs. In Chennai, the former city of Madras, which I remembered having once heard about from my middle school social studies teacher – a balding man who thanks to the long tufts of hair on either side of his head had resembled nothing if not a medieval soldier fleeing the battlefield – the air was unbelievably dirty, just as in every other rapidly urbanised city in India. Nonetheless, the faintest smell of the sea, wafting everywhere over this noisy and cut-throat city, helped to soften that impression, even if only by a small fraction. During the interview in Tokyo, the vice president, Mr Karthikeyan, had told me that Chennai was situated by the sea, with the Bay of Bengal to the east, remarking that the weather didn't get particularly hot in summer. That was certainly true as far as the map was concerned, but when I laid eyes on this cluttered city, I couldn't help but feel sceptical. Was there really a beach near all this?

And so came the third day of the flood.

Pulling back the curtains in the light of early morning, I finally spotted ground. I grabbed my bag, and as the elevator still wasn't working, ran down the staircase at the side of the building. Not having left my apartment for three whole days, I wanted nothing more than to touch that ground, whether it was covered in mud or not, to plant myself on it one step at a time, first with my right foot, then with my left, savouring the tactile sensations. Now that I was outside, I started making my way to the office. Although not directly adjacent to the Adyar, both my apartment and my workplace lay in the course of the river. My office was on the second floor, but still I found myself wondering if it might not have been submerged.

The first thing that struck me when I stepped out into the street was the smell. A heavy, sour, sweet odour, the smell of the morning after the first flood of my life. Lining either side of the roads that crossed the residential area were piles of muddy trash, objects that in past lives had been carpets, mattresses, checked shirts, school shorts, saris, sandals, torn tree branches, rats, the stuffed polar bear toys in their bright red vests that guarded the entrance to many a Christian household here in Chennai, Spider-Man action figures, and a plethora of so many more disparate names. A viscous, cloying scent rose up from each of these items crouching on the side of the road, wrapping itself around me as I walked by them, their merciless sounds permeating every pore of my body. I must have let my mind wander for a few seconds, as I ended up stumbling over something. I caught hold of a nearby tree as I waited for the night to clear from my darkened vision.

'Oh, are you alright?'

When I raised my face, a white-haired woman in a sari was standing before me. She was holding a pack of milk in her right hand and a bag filled with tomatoes and okra in her left.

'I'm okay,' I answered reflexively.

'Take care,' the woman said with a gentle smile and a dip of the head, as per the local custom.

Something wasn't right, I thought, my head still clouded as I hurried in the direction of my workplace.

I stepped off 100 Feet Road and approached the Adyar River, my path becoming increasingly difficult to navigate as the street edged uphill toward the bridge. I laid eyes on the huge sari-covered behind of a woman tugging at a child's hand, an old man with a cane, three young men walking with their arms slung around each other's shoulders. Catching glimpses through the gaps between countless heads and shoulders up ahead, I realised that an incredible crowd had assembled over on the bridge.

People from all over were gathering to witness the massed detritus of this once-in-a-century flood.

My company was on the left bank of the river, which meant that the only way to reach it was by crossing the bridge. Normally it would have taken me only a minute or two to cross to the far side and another fifteen or so to climb the nearby slope. As I let my attention wander, my gaze drifted over the handrail on my left to the road below. Amid the stores lining the muddy street leading to the bank – a tool shop, a paint merchant, a fruit juice stand, a motorcycle shop emblazoned with a large signboard for the Japanese company Yamaha – appeared an open-air coconut seller from which the dull thud of a hatchet sounded out at regular intervals, while customers sitting in the shade of a tree slurped up the contents of the huge fruits with plastic straws. I was trying not to remember that there was a public toilet located next to the brown water, when I almost tripped over the steps at my feet. At long last, I had reached the approach to the bridge.

Still being violently jostled by a crowd positively raring with excitement, I managed to peer over the handrail at my side and was left stunned by the sight of the ochre-coloured torrent raging around the bridge piers, having risen to a level that I had never seen before.

Outside of the annual onslaught of the rainy season, the Adyar was a typical urban drainage channel. Each time that I crossed the bridge, I would be assaulted by the rancid odour of putrefaction, and if I blinked my eyes, I would be able to make out huge mounds of garbage scattered all over the riverbank, along with small bodies of greenish-grey water stagnating on either side of the sandbar. It seemed that with every passing day, huge quantities of untreated sewage from the five-million-plus inhabitants of Chennai poured into the city's three main rivers and canals, the Adyar included, before twisting and turning and tumbling into the Bay of Bengal. At least for the time being, I had no intention of consuming any fish during my stay here. Nonetheless, every now and then, I would see flocks of birds gliding over the water before coming to perch on the sandbars, or the occasional cluster of purple water hyacinths bobbing along the surface, and those sights would fill me with the unmistakable impression that this river was the true lifeblood of the neighbourhood.

Now, after the flood, as I stared out over the bridge, the water's joyful passage through the area was as clear as day. A wide roadway ran down the centre of the path ahead of me, surrounded on either side by a pair of sidewalks, along which was a layer of mud around a metre wide and fifty centimetres high, stretching from end to end of the more than five-hundred-metre-long concrete bridge. The sheer volume of mud and accumulated detritus that the bridge had captured was rich with the very history of the city. It must have taken dozens of labourers hours to rake it all to one side, but the first flood in a hundred years meant that all the junk and debris that had lain buried for the better part of a century had been brought now to the light of day. The mud of a century, stirred up from the unimaginable depths of the drainage channels that crossed the city, churned and crushed together until it became a testament to the land itself.

At this point, the sticky, mouldering smell that had been lingering ever since I ventured out into the city streets reached its peak, its true source revealed as this accumulated mud. The smell of the morning after the flood completely permeated my senses – enough, it seemed, to make me feel like surrendering my body and soul. But where on earth could I go? Just as my thoughts started to drift away, a forty-something-year-old woman in a yellow sari stepped out in front of me, and with no warning, thrust her hand deep into the mountain of claggy muck.

'What are you doing in a place like this?' she cried, using her free hand to violently douse the retrieved mass with water, before wiping it down with her neck scarf to reveal a boy maybe five years of age.

The woman brushed her frayed hair to one side, then clicked her tongue in annoyance. 'Dinakaran! Where do you think you've been these past seven years? Making your parents worry so!'

The child began to wail as his mother pulled him along by the ear, the pair of them soon disappearing into the milling crowd.

Then, behind me, came a man's voice. 'Aiyoh! Jaikumar? *This* is where you've been sleeping?'

I glanced over my shoulder to find four burly limbs sticking out from the mire as two men, probably in their sixties and dressed in turmeric-coloured loincloths, helped a mud-caked figure, his eyes blinking in bewilderment, to his feet. 'Just how long are you planning to sleep there?' one of them asked in exasperation. The two heaved him out onto the pavement, revealing a young man more than a hundred and ninety centimetres in height. I was amazed that a body like that had managed to stay buried for so long.

'Haven't you let the teacher thump you enough for falling asleep in class?'

'That's right, Jai. Don't you remember our writing teacher, Mr Balraj?'

I watched as the young man, coated in mud, still yawning and wearing an embarrassed grin, joined shoulders with his two greying shirtless companions. They should have been too far apart in age to be on such close terms, but the three of them beamed with the joy of a long-awaited reunion.

'What do you say we go see a movie? Haven't been to the cinema in a while.'

'Your mum never stopped looking for you. But she died a decade ago now.'

'Your wife remarried in less than a year though.'

The three of them burst out into breathless laughter, their shoulders convulsing as they disappeared into the crowd.

Why did I feel as if I could understand what everyone around me was saying? Only yesterday, I hadn't been able to comprehend a word of Tamil, but no sooner had that smell just now left me feeling faint-headed than a strange sensation seemed to have fallen over me. Naturally, I should have asked myself whether the scent of this hundred-year-old mud might not have something to do with what I was experiencing, but before I could even pause to gather my thoughts, I was stopped in my tracks as another voice sounded behind me in Japanese. 'Good morning, Sensei.'

I recognised the speaker at once, and even before I could fully turn round, I was already fed up to my back teeth with Devaraj, the corners of his mouth puckered in his usual faint smile.

He was one of the students in my Japanese class, yet he was dressed not in the shirt and slacks that he always wore to the office, but rather a simple T-shirt and a short loincloth like those worn by road construction workers. In his hands, he was grasping a tool similar in design to a bamboo rake. Maybe he was working to help clean the bridge? In any event, I couldn't just ignore him.

'Good morning, Devaraj-san,' I said in Japanese. 'What are you doing?'

'I do penalty work for a traffic error,' he answered.

'You're *doing* penalty work,' I corrected him.

Right, right, I remembered, there was a system in Tamil Nadu by which people might be required to pay for traffic violations through community service. One of the human resources staff had said something to that effect when a student didn't turn up to class one day.

Devaraj certainly wasn't an easy student to deal with. Two weeks after I had started teaching in the company's Japanese language training program, I had developed a bald spot around the size of a ten-yen coin on the top of my head, at least eight yen of which was due to this young man.

For example, there was the first time that I had taught ideographic kanji characters in class. Hoping to demonstrate that each character has its own inherent meaning, I wrote the character for *like* on the whiteboard.

'This kanji character is made up of two parts. The left side is the same as the character for *woman*, the right side that for *child*. Women *like* children, you see.' I pointed once more to the character on the whiteboard. 'And so the meaning of this character is *like*.'

'Sensei,' Devaraj called out, raising his hand without so much as a moment's delay. 'I took the train yesterday. It was very crowded. There were two blind girls, children, standing all the way. There was a woman sitting in front of them. But she didn't give her seat to the girls. So she doesn't like children.'

This was in English, of course, but I couldn't understand why he would bring up this anecdote in the middle of my explanation of kanji characters. Yet it was certainly true that the chaos of Chennai's transportation and road networks during rush hour defied the imagination, to the extent that many company executives preferred to fly to work to avoid the traffic. Indeed, ever since I had come to live in Chennai, such scenes had become a familiar sight.

I would arrive at the building at around nine o'clock each morning, and on most days, the temperature would already be well in excess of thirty degrees. Usually, just before the clock struck the hour, a man, the vice president, would step in front of me as he took off his aerial wings.

'Good morning,' he said, raising a hand in amicable greeting.

He adjusted the collar of his tasteful blue shirt, stacked his wings together, and threw them over his shoulder. The attendant caught them just before they could hit the ground, and with a fluid, practised motion, ferried them off to the wing drying area in the corner of the parking lot.

Shortly before coming to India, I met an Osaka girl at an udon noodle restaurant in Ikebukuro. She claimed that I resembled her late aunt and quickly took to addressing me as *Auntie.* Anyway, as I dragged my oversized luggage behind me on my way to board my flight to India, I received a text message from her. *Auntie, did you know? Indian people fly these days. I saw it on YouTube.* Ah, I thought, this must be the famed Osakan sense of humour on show – but while walking to the office the very next day, I saw with my very own eyes that people truly were flying.

Hindu Technologies has offices in Tokyo, Osaka and Fukuoka, and Mr Karthikeyan, the vice president, once served as the manager of the Fukuoka branch. He had a proficient grasp of Japanese, even if he did occasionally mangle his honorifics, and his features were crisp and well-organised, hinting at a strongly masculine face back in his youth. Carefully patting down his half-silver hair brought into disorder by his morning flight, he turned to me and asked, 'How are you today?'

'I'm managing,' I answered vaguely, shifting my gaze to the parking lot where the wing drying area shone brightly in the morning sun. There was a giant banana tree growing nearby, positioned so that it would receive constant light no matter the time of day. Needless to say, an attendant was always on hand to hastily retrieve the many pairs of wings hanging on its branches in the event of a sudden downpour.

As I exchanged greetings with Mr Karthikeyan, another executive descended at a steep incline, and upon alighting, reached behind his back with both hands, the middle and ring fingers of each adorned with thick gold rings, quickly removed his flying equipment, and cast both wings aside as if they were no more than spent cigarette butts.

Next to the banana tree, a space had been set aside for employees to enjoy tea and snacks. Drawn by the enticing aroma, I couldn't help but turn my head to see the sari-clad cooks busy preparing milk tea and banana fritters for the employees' breakfast in a simple kitchen comprising a cutting board and a gas burner set on a long benchtop. There was no such thing as winter in southern India, and as such, the branches of the banana tree overhead were always overflowing with fresh fruit regardless of the season. I was fascinated by the sight before me, of everyone working together so efficiently, dividing the various tasks among themselves – peeling the fruit, cutting them lengthwise into thin slices on the cutting board, battering and frying them, and making tea for those employees who came for breakfast. In South India, bananas are considered truly providential – the unripe fruit is used to make fritters, the ripened fruit eaten raw, the flowers used in curries, the stems in salads, and the leaves for serving and to make tableware.

'Well, I have a meeting in a few minutes,' said Mr Karthikeyan in the smooth voice of a busy executive. He nodded with his chin to the security guard waiting at the elevator door, flashed me a debonair smile, and then quickly disappeared into the building.

After that, more and more executives continued to land in the parking lot, and the attendant diligently collected each one's wings in turn, hanging them carefully on the branches of the banana tree so that they wouldn't overlap and would be shaded from direct sunlight. The road conditions in Chennai are unimaginable, and the number of people engaging in reckless flying, especially in the mornings and evenings, had reached such a level that just last year a system had been put in place to restrict flying by aerial wing to the privileged classes. I could only imagine the utter devastation that must have occurred on a daily basis before the change in policy.

A couple of weeks before, the vice president of Hindu Technologies sent an advertisement for a Japanese language instructor to my ex-husband's company, and during my interview, after I had applied on my ex's heavy-handed recommendation, he had asked only a few incredibly simple questions, such as *Have you ever been to India?* and *Are you in good health?* He didn't bother to confirm even the most basic of details, not even my knowledge of and experience in Japanese language education or my qualifications. The simple fact of that matter was that I knew nothing at all about it, and I didn't have any qualifications to speak of.

It was possible to obtain a certificate as a Japanese language teacher by completing a language education course at a university, by taking a Japanese language instructor training course, or by passing the Japanese Language Teaching Competency Test – but needless to say, at that point in time, I hadn't even been aware of this simple fact.

Hindu Technologies frequently transferred or assigned staff to its three branch offices in Japan, conducted weekly meetings with Japanese business partners over Skype, and provided countless opportunities for Japanese clients to visit the head office. As such, the company had started a Japanese language training program for its employees a few years ago, but apparently all the real Japanese language teachers who had been hired quit after only a year or so, and as such, management had decided that it would be good enough just to learn from native speakers. Having now found myself in this country, I was naturally impressed by India's five-thousand-year-long history, but of course, I still had to taste daily my own personal karmic perdition.

According to some schools of Buddhism, erring monks are at risk of being cast down into one of three distinct hells – but for a half-hearted teacher, hell is nothing other than the classroom itself.

When I first arrived in Chennai and walked through the doors of my new place of employment, I found two thick volumes of a textbook called *Minna no Nihongo – Japanese for Everyone* – along with an accompanying English-language reference book in the office cabinet on the second floor. Later, I read online that this was the most popular textbook used in Japanese language education for speakers of other languages. The English reference book contained translations of sentences and vocabulary from the textbooks, along with English explanations of most major grammar points. As I rifled through the shelves, my eyes scanning their contents in a bloodshot frenzy, I came across a supplementary reader that looked to have been used by one of the previous teachers. In essence, it was a guidebook filled with various tips for language instructors, but as I didn't have time to study it at a more leisurely pace, I ended up staying back in the office until late at night, skimming through it and jotting down anything that I might be able to teach the students on the sheets of printing paper that I had been given by the human resources department, marking them up in red, black, and blue to put together a lesson plan for my first day of classes. Since I couldn't speak Tamil, I would have to use English as an intermediary language, at least until my students were capable of understanding simple Japanese expressions, and so I had to prepare all the grammar and vocabulary explanations ahead of time. From that moment forward, I embarked on a precarious hand-to-mouth routine of first drawing up my lesson plans the night before, then keeping them always in the corner of my vision as I put them into practice the following day. Devaraj must have recognised my lack of experience during the very first lesson, must have sensed at once that I wasn't at all worthy of the class's respect.

It didn't take long for him to grasp the personalities of the other group members and to establish himself as lord over his domain. My students would ignore me no matter how many times I told them in tired exasperation to please be quiet, yet all it took was a tongue-in-cheek click of Devaraj's tongue to make the room fall silent, as though doused in a bucketful of cold water.

He might have had an eye-catching mien, the kind that could even prompt a double look, but it was clear from his general conduct and from his occasionally vulgar facial expressions that he was far and away the worst student in the class.

For example, during my first grammar quiz, I had sat at the teacher's desk at the front of the room where I should have been able to closely monitor the students, but I was so busy working on my lesson plans that I didn't pay any attention to the class at all. When I glanced up, I was just quick enough to catch Devaraj exchanging glances with the student sitting by his side as he returned his answer sheet to his desk. I was convinced that he had helped a poorly performing classmate to cheat on his paper, but I hadn't been able to make it out clearly enough to be absolutely sure. As such, I stared across at them both in silence, but without a moment's delay, Devaraj fixed me with such a fierce look that I ended up averting my gaze.

There were only seven students in the class, all men, a number quickly reduced to six after I had one dismissed, and apart from Devaraj, they all seemed to come from families that, although perhaps not particularly wealthy, had the means to provide their children with a solid university education. In India, university students usually complete their studies in May, so after being hired by Hindu Technologies as new graduates, my students had been instructed to learn Japanese for four months before being assigned to their roles in the company, and so had awaited my arrival in August. Naturally, some of my future students wouldn't be fresh graduates, and when the time came for them to be ordered to participate in the Japanese language training program, they would be required to take time off from their usual responsibilities at the end of a given project to spend the next four months struggling with a new language.

My students were completely different from those who might attend a Japanese language school at their own expense, perhaps with the goal of one day finding a job in Japan or in the hope of meeting a Japanese woman unable to speak English or Tamil. Hindu Technologies' policy was to hire its own Japanese language teachers, provide textbooks, notebooks, and other necessary teaching materials, and of course, pay its staff to learn Japanese for four months while receiving a full salary. Yet my students were like high schoolers, with the mental age of teenagers, completely ignorant of the real purpose of an employee education funded at the company's expense, of how this experience might affect the future trajectories of their careers or lives. Worst of all, they had far too lofty opinions of themselves.

'This class is for learning Japanese, so please don't speak in Tamil or English,' I remonstrated. But no matter how many times I reminded or cautioned them, the happy-go-lucky team before me just wouldn't listen.

For example, I once tried asking Ananda the following: 'What do we call a *transitive verb* in Japanese?'

With an innocent glance over his shoulder, he consulted with Devaraj in Tamil, before, showing not the slightest hint of guilt or embarrassment, answering '*Tadoshi*.'

'*Tadōshi*!' Devaraj corrected him from behind, stretching out the long vowel.

Devaraj had a habit of mimicking me, especially the way that I corrected the students when they mixed their long and short vowels, and of exploding into guffaws of wild laughter with the abruptness of a bubble bursting open.

So passed a long ninety minutes of torment, until finally I was saved by the sound of my own voice saying 'Let's take a break, everyone.'

I staggered out of the classroom at eleven o'clock. Classes were held between nine thirty in the morning and five forty-five in the evening, with a lunch break in the middle and a further fifteen-minute break in both morning and afternoon, with each session running for around an hour and a half.

The constant back and forth between offence and defence in front of the whiteboard had left me beleaguered, and after being on my feet for a full ninety minutes, I all but crawled back to my office. 'Tea, please,' I said to the receptionist as I glanced over my empty desk, and the sturdy-looking woman nodded my way as she picked up the extension phone. During the designated break times, tea was prepared in the lounge on the fourth floor, and the regular employees would make their way there one by one if they wanted a drink. For the executives, however, a girl would bring their drinks directly to their offices. I might have ostensibly been treated as an executive, but I was clearly less important than the managers and section chiefs, and I almost always had to ask for tea to be brought to me if I hoped to ever receive it. Incidentally, in South India, tea is called *thee* instead of *chai*, and in a further difference from North India, coffee is also an option, with the local varieties of both beverages sharing the characteristic property of being extremely sweet.

The receptionist hung up the handset and tilted her head to one side to indicate that the drink was on its way. Her mannerism struck me as remarkably similar to that of a white beckoning cat figure with startled eyes sitting atop a red cushion, its right paw raised, clutching in its left an old-fashioned golden *koban* coin like those used in the Edo period, emblazoned with the words *Ten Million Rupees in Debt.*

On that subject, the Osaka girl whom I met at the udon restaurant in Ikebukuro sent me a text message the week after I arrived in Chennai: *Auntie! It's terrible! All the beckoning cat figures in Osaka have disappeared! And I saw something else in front of a kelp store on the shopping street in Shinsaibashi, some kind of fancy elephant statue!*

I had been so busy preparing for my move to India that I hadn't really been paying much attention to the news, but I did recall hearing that the cities of Chennai and Osaka had recently signed a friendship cooperation agreement, and that all the beckoning cat figures in Osaka were to be temporarily exchanged for all the Ganesha statues in Chennai. The trade had been carried out in the dead of night by goodwill envoys sent from each city, and so the statue of Ganesha that had been standing guard outside the offices of Hindu Technologies ever since the company moved into its present building three years ago could now be found in the Osaka City Hall in Nakanoshima, standing watch next to a television screen over the lobby on the second floor, while a beckoning cat figure that had once made its home atop the food ticket vending machine in the same building's cafeteria had likewise been relocated to the entrance of my new company's headquarters. As per South Indian custom, a thick garland of flowers, half yellow and half almond pink, now hung around the cat's neck, while its right paw next to its face was adorned with a lotus bracelet. The other side of the exchange, Ganesha, is a Hindu deity who brings wealth and wisdom, and has long been enshrined in stores all over India as a god of business prosperity, even in stores run by Muslims who otherwise forbid idolatry. Moreover, since Ganesha is known for his power to remove all obstacles, figures of him are a standard feature on the dashboards of Indian cars. Right now, you could find a beckoning cat figure sitting atop its red cushion even on the dashboard of the vice president's Lexus, its body polished so thoroughly that the odd employee might occasionally pause in front of their reflection for a minute to fix their hair. The vice president, whose responsibilities included entertaining

Japanese clients who came to visit Chennai, always had a chauffeur-driven car on standby in the company parking lot to pick up important clients and drop them off at the airport, or to take them out sightseeing or for meals. I can't remember when exactly it was, but when I pointed out the beckoning cat figure to him, he said only, 'That little kitty has been living in my car for a good while now.'

A quick addition: custom says that cats beckoning with their right paws invite money, while those that beckon with their left paws summon people. Yet it seems that a fair number of left-handed beckoning cats have inexplicably started raising their right paws since coming to India, while right-handed ones have shifted to lifting their left paws, quite as if they have all taken to raising both paws in unreserved joy since arriving here.

By the way, I mentioned earlier that my students had the mental age of teenagers, but when I asked them in class how old they all were, they responded, almost to a person, 'Twenty-one.'

I was taken aback somewhat by their responses. Only Muruganantham, who had completed a master's degree, was twenty-three, while Vishnu, whose older brother, a brilliant engineer working at the Kanagawa branch of a famous IT company, replied coolly, 'Twenty.'

I would have expected university graduates to be at least twenty-two or twenty-three. 'Isn't university in India four years?' I tried asking, only to be told that it was normal here for people to misrepresent their children's ages when sending them to kindergarten, passing them off as four years of age when they were really just three, and that from there, they would enter elementary school at the age of five when they were supposed to be six. Only wealthy families who wanted to give their children a head start learning English tended to send their children to kindergarten. Vishnu, who had somehow managed to start his school life at the age of four, responded for the whole class when he said, 'Sensei. This is the entrance requirement for elementary schools in India.' With that, he raised his right hand, wrapped it behind his head and, pinched the lobe of his left ear. The reason, he told me, was that infants under the age of five had short arms and large heads, and so were unable to perform this action. I couldn't help but feel that he was putting one over me, but in a country without a family registry system, maybe that really was good enough? Still, with a very Japanese sensibility, I asked simply, 'Why do Indian parents *want* to send their children off to school so early?'

Looking at me with as if I was failing to see the blindingly obvious, my students answered as one. 'Because then they can graduate sooner and start work.'

A great many parents may be moved to tears to hear this, but in India, it seems that one's wages are paid to their parents up until they get married. My students claimed that those who are yet to leave home give their wages to their parents in full while those who live in apartments of their own hand over everything except for housing expenses when they go back to visit once or twice a month, from which they then receive a small allowance. Not only that, it isn't at all unusual for university students still living with their parents to tutor groups of children from their local neighbourhoods to earn spending money. Indeed, I often saw pamphlets around my own apartment advertising tuition services for five hundred rupees per month. India is a passionate country when it comes to education, with extracurricular tuition fees for elementary school students set at three hundred rupees a month, while those for high school students are around five hundred – a university student's charge for watching over the neighbourhood children practically every day. Of course, this custom is a direct reflection of an attitude held by many an Indian parent, that as they paid for their children's education from elementary school through to university, they deserve to be repaid in kind – which perhaps also explains Indian morals. I couldn't help but be struck with admiration whenever I was confronted with such examples of stolid Indian-style rationality.

And that wasn't my only cause for admiration. Whenever a student was unable to attend class for some unavoidable reason, they would contact me early in the morning with the most remarkable of explanations. 'I crashed my motorbike dodging a cow,' they might say, or 'My father fainted,' or 'My sister is getting her ears pierced today.'

After two weeks of struggling to manage the class, in consultation with the head of the human resources department, I decided to dismiss the student who had cheated on his first grammar quiz by copying Devaraj's answers and had continued to perform poorly thereafter, and resolved to expel Devaraj too.

However, what forced me to ultimately give up on this idea was Devaraj's extraordinary Japanese language ability. He was a fast learner, quick to comprehend, his memory beyond impressive, and while he couldn't use most new grammar patterns immediately upon learning them, he had a much firmer sense of their nuances than the other members of the class. It was clear that if I kicked him out, the group as a whole would suffer for it.

In fact, the reason why I couldn't be too firm in my remonstrations for the students to be quiet was that those with limited comprehension ability often turned to Devaraj to supplement my poor explanations with his own commentary. In other words, unable to follow my English, they turned to him asking, 'What, what, what did she say?' and only thanks to his explanations did they finally grasp what I had intended to convey.

Nonetheless, unlike the other students, Devaraj would always be leaning slouched down in his chair, oftentimes yawning indiscreetly with his hands folded behind his head, picking at his nose or else staring back at me with an expression that suggested I was treating him like an idiot. At such times, I couldn't help but rue the fact that I hadn't dismissed him from the class when I had had the chance.

On the other hand, whenever an individual of note came to visit us, his attitude would undergo a complete one-eighty. For instance, when the vice president, Mr Karthikeyan, dropped into the classroom with a photographer to take some pictures for the company newsletter, Devaraj would turn unexpectedly meek and quiet, obsequious even, a living embodiment of that hackneyed Japanese expression a *borrowed cat*, hands rested firmly on his knees, back straight, his face aglow with a winning smile while his usual wry grin would be nowhere to be seen.

'Together, in a loud voice, everyone,' I would ask, and at such times, there would be no stopping him from repeating the numerous example sentences that we had learned, phrases such as *I like curd rice!* or *More sambal, please!* or *What would you do with a hundred million yen?*

Curd rice, incidentally, is a chaotic porridge-like dish, pure white in colour, made by mixing rice with fermented milk, and can be found in practically every Tamil restaurant, while sambal is a kind of soup filled with vegetables like tomatoes, beans, onions, and eggplant.

No sooner did Mr Karthikeyan and the cameraman leave than I wrote the word *betsujin* on the whiteboard, explaining that it meant *another person* with the example sentence *He was like another person just now.* Devaraj seemed to catch on, as his handsome lips curled at the edges, but I couldn't help but notice that his smile was a little different from usual.

In any event, I didn't want to pursue the matter further. For all that I was aware, this kaleidoscopic changeability of his could have been the result of a hard life known only to him. But all the same, the world certainly wasn't so fickle as to look forgivingly on that attitude of his.

At that moment, a man in the thin, khaki-coloured uniform like that of a police officer emerged from the congestion on the bridge, teeming like a crowded fairground, and scolded Devaraj in a strident tone of voice. 'Hey! Just what do you think you're doing?! You had better be taking this seriously, you hear?'

The traffic police supervisor had caught him slacking off, and so Devaraj hurried to push his rake through the hundred-year-old mud covering the sidewalk. The ridges of mud offered no resistance as the rake sank into them. All of a sudden, Devaraj's hand, perhaps having made contact with something, came to a stop, and he wrenched the rake out with all his might.

As soon as I saw it, my instincts kicked in – pulling back hard from the inescapable throng of people, I managed to half extricate myself from the confusion just long enough to lean down and scoop up the object, scraping off the mud until I laid eyes on a bottle of whiskey. Suntory Yamazaki Twelve Years Old. There was something written on the label in black marker pen. Leaning close, I could just make out my ex-husband's name, along with the words *father's fury*, a line from a short satirical poem. My ex-husband always kept several bottles of liquor alongside his snacks, but they were usually just small Daruma bottles. There seemed to be something inside it, but when I gave it a shake, I could tell that it was empty. Of all possible items to dig up here, why did it have to be something that brought back so many troubling memories?

In general, whether a class, a queue or a promise, I'm not particularly fond of things that end up stretching out for too long.

When it comes to plants, I don't like long, spindly vines either. I prefer the kinds of grasses and flowers that grow close to the ground, like chickweed or stitchwort. In fact, I have a little story about those two.

I'm not related to my father by blood. When I was five years old, my mother lost her husband, and she met my father shortly afterwards. It wasn't long before the two moved in together, and no sooner did the legal period of prohibition of remarriage expire than they made it official. This was my new father's second marriage too, but unlike my mother, he had no other children. After marrying my mother, he lost his job as a bank subcontractor, and so resolving to find a new employer as soon as possible, he managed to land a position in the debt collection department of a financial institution. The company described his role as *loan renegotiation*, but in truth, he was simply a debt collector. My father occasionally took me with him on his *renegotiations*. It all started one day when my mother came down with such a bad cold that my father was left with no other choice but to take me with him, but he quickly realised that bringing along a small child had the curious effect of increasing his collection rate. I would have preferred to stay with my mother, but I didn't dislike my father, and as a child, I had my own sense of mission and duty.

It was so long ago now that I can hardly remember much from that time any more, but I do recall one particular afternoon out on assignment. I once read in a book with a blue cover that if you borrow too much money from people, your brain can end up filled with a substance that smells almost like lotus honey. Looking back, that man who had borrowed far too much money, the debt collector who had come to retrieve it, and the latter's companion too may all have experienced that afternoon in the one shared dream.

The reason why I can remember it is that it was my first time going out with the watch that my father had given me as a birthday present the day before. It had a pink dial with an illustration of my favourite children's characters – the Little Twin Stars – dancing on it, and the long and short hands were shaped like magic wands.

'What time is it?' my father asked again and again as the train made its way through the suburbs, and even though I didn't actually need to check, I would always gladly make a show of glancing down at the watch face on my left wrist.

'It's three… twenty-five!' I remember answering with excitement, despite not usually being much of a talker.

Our destination was far from the station, and my father and I walked in silence. Before I knew it, we entered a dense forest that prompted me to wonder if we were truly still in the suburbs of Tokyo, and after stepping on a succession of colourful mushrooms, ferns, and blankets of moss, we finally passed through an intricate grove of trees and reached a field of open flowers.

A narrow path ran through the centre of that field, leading to what looked like a house on the far side. The debtor's home with its slanting grimy red roof tiles seemed to absorb the bright afternoon sunlight.

My father and I stepped out onto the path as though wading into a sea of flowers. In front of me, the waves of blossoms were unceasing, their wicks swirling around me in an ever-stronger vortex, opening up one after the next in rapid succession. I had never seen such a vast swathe of flowers, and I felt my vision blurring, until at some point, my father turned round suddenly and stumbled into the mass of colour to my right.

From amid that suffocating whirlpool, he reached down, and without warning, pulled up by the ear a man around fifty years of age. 'Mr Kitamura. I'm with Eikō Credit. We spoke over the phone yesterday.'

'I'll return the money tomorrow. I'll check the balance again tomorrow,' the man mumbled with an earphone dangling from his other ear.

'The Nikkei Stock average on the Tokyo Stock Exchange has just rebounded for the first time in three days… Compared to previous sessions… This should be the biggest gain this year…'

The stock market, it seemed, was still exerting its hold over the man's body and soul.

'The parent company's stock should have risen enough to cover it all by tomorrow… I'm sure of it… Tomorrow morning…' he continued to whisper.

The debtor, Kitamura, had previously worked simultaneously both as a boutique designer and as a home interior decorator in Tokyo. My father was already used to his unique mimicry skills, as Kitamura had attempted an eccentric form of evasion during his last visit, dressing himself up in clothes the same pattern as the wallpaper and standing motionless in front of a wall inside pretending not to be home.

My father dusted away the flowers from his clothes with both hands. 'I have a better idea, Mr Kitamura.'

His proposal was a well-worn trick, to take advantage of Kitamura's still dazed state to take him to another money lender, and should he be successful in taking out another loan, to make him repay at least the interest to this one on the spot. No sooner did they reach an agreement than together the three of us turned back the way that we had come.

We passed through the forest again, Kitamura and my father walking side by side while I tagged along behind, once more treading atop the carpet of moss in the dim light. At one point during that gloomy journey, I felt a slight irritation on my wrist. I quickly glanced down at my left hand, but there was nothing to see. The discomfort, however, continued, and when I raised my wrist once again, a crimson sausage, almost as thick as my wrist itself, dangled down in front of me.

I let out a scream at the top of my lungs, which must have startled my father, as he turned back to face me. 'Ah, it's a leech. You've been bitten by a leech.' He immediately grabbed hold of my left hand, tore the leech off from the root of its head, and threw it away.

The creature had hidden itself beneath the band of my Little Twin Stars watch, draining my blood for however long it took me to have that belated reaction. I was so shocked that my heart kept on racing, and I continued to sniffle on the verge of tears until we arrived home. Of course, I had nightmares about the incident for three nights in a row. Ever since, I've practically had a phobia of long spindly things in general, to the point where I can't even stand the name of the famous manga artist Ebisu Yoshikazu, seeing as his name is written with the characters for *leech* and *child*.

Anyway, as I said earlier, I have no prejudices against the business of debt collection, and I first met my ex-husband when I responded to an advert for a part-time job as an office clerk.

We were married in less than six months, and while out on a walk one beautiful morning after a night of rain, I spotted a nice moist plot of soil between the Seiyu supermarket in front of the station and the pachinko parlour next door. I couldn't resist the urge to go play in the dirt and leave my footprints. All of a sudden I noticed someone waving to me through the window of the Doutor café on the first floor of the supermarket building.

Shielding my eyes against the light, I realised that hers was a familiar face. When I entered, the face was already waiting at the counter, saying to the cashier, 'My friend will have a coffee too.' It all happened so fast that I missed my chance to point out that I would have preferred tea.

She was a woman in her sixties and had been introduced to countless jobs by a dispatch company operating from the same building as my husband's business.

'Hey, don't set me up with any in-store food sampling placements, alright? Supermarkets are always filled with young mums letting their kids run wild, getting 'em to sample sausages like a bunch of idiots. They keep coming back for more and more, and when you tell 'em to make sure their kids are eating properly at home, they go and complain to the manager about you. I can't handle it.'

After that, the company decided that housekeeping would be within the narrow list of possibilities that she could handle, and now she seemed to have a job cleaning a love hotel a few stations away on a private railway line three or four times a week. Apparently, she had just finished her night shift there. She was a typical chain smoker, and she continued to add more to the ashtray already piled high with spent butts as she rambled on about how she was looking for a new job, complaining that the pay at the love hotel was too low while vegetables were so expensive these days, going on and on asking how on earth could a Chinese cabbage possibly cost three hundred yen, when without warning, her voice dropped several decibels, and she said, 'You should keep an eye on that husband of yours.'

Early that morning she had seen my husband leaving the love hotel where she worked. Perhaps the café was a little warm for her, as she loosened the scarf around her neck when she lit up another cigarette. 'That man, he's got himself a beautiful young wife, but still he can't help himself.'

She breathed out a puff of smoke toward the ceiling, that mannerism drawing my attention to the faint lip hair beneath her nose.

If this was the beginning of the tale, what added further weight to it was the testimony of the proprietress of a bar that my husband frequented. My husband had already taken me to said bar on several occasions, so I immediately made my way there to see for myself whether what the in-store-food-sample-hating woman had told me was indeed true.

'I heard the Tanakas are having a bit of a spat. Apparently the missus found a membership card for a love hotel in her husband's wallet, and when she called them, they gave up his entire usage history. She's even gone to a lawyer, they say,' the proprietress soon told me.

'And then there's Mr Suzuki. I heard he had a call girl brought to his room at a business hotel, only for her to end up being his mother-in-law.'

'Do you know Mr Takahashi? Apparently his wife's phone rang while she was taking a bath, and when he picked up, a man's voice asked, "What are your plans for tomorrow?" Before he knew it, he found himself answering, "Filing my tax return. It's that time of the year again."'

The proprietress had a tendency to reveal the secrets of all her regular customers, and I had come here fully anticipating that through her characteristic lack of discretion, I would learn everything that I needed to know.

As such, it wasn't all that difficult extracting the testimony of this broad-faced woman, and as soon as I started fishing for information while she fixed a watered-down whiskey for another customer, she said, 'He came here around a week ago, your husband…'

She went on to give me a detailed account of how my husband, a regular patron of the bar, after becoming unusually drunk, blurted out the following. Apparently, an old girlfriend of his, now married, had suddenly reached out hoping to meet him with a most unusual line. 'I'm going to have a hysterectomy, and I'd like to see you before the surgery.' They say that there is nothing longer in this world than the uterus, that said organ is capable of stretching not only to the very ends of the earth, but to the ends of time as well, that it stretches on seemingly forever, haunting people, drawing them in, and ultimately shackling them in place.

Anyway, I didn't want to have to be the one to break up with my husband over his extra-marital affair, and so for the time being I decided to take advantage of another man who had for a good many months been intermittently trying to ask me out. The man was a strange fellow, a social studies teacher at a private high school in Tokyo whose greatest pleasures in life were horse racing and karaoke, and he had a longstanding habit of using black-market lending because he didn't want his information to be registered with the Japan Credit Information Reference Centre. He popped up one day in the reception room at my husband's company after seeing it marketed alongside the adult entertainment advertisements in a weekly horse racing magazine, then returned several more times afterward, and on each occasion he would ask me out while my husband wasn't looking. No sooner did I learn of my husband's infidelity from the proprietress than I accepted the man's next invitation to go to a small bar with him, where he forced me to sing the classic song 'I Still Miss My Ex' in a duet with him. When next I saw him, he handed me a CD of 'You Can Forget About Me' and instructed me to memorise the lyrics for our second outing.

I had no intention of drilling the words to the song into my brain, but the following day I went back to that proprietress's bar with the man and emptied a bottle of Suntory Yamazaki Twelve Years Old that my husband had apparently gone out and splurged on.

'The Japanese language teacher has gone on maternity leave, so like that, I've had responsibility for supervising the student haiku club foisted on me,' the high school teacher said as he shook the bottle upside down, pouring the remaining whiskey into a glass and stirring it with a muddler.

'Do you have to write haiku too?' I asked.

'Not all the time, but every now and then they kick up a fuss if I don't. I'm not cut out for it, but them's the breaks.'

He must have been particularly drunk when he borrowed a black marker pen from the bar proprietress and started scribbling on the empty bottle:

Tōsan no	how frightening
tatari osoroshii	father's curse of repayment
tosan kana	thirty in ten

I couldn't remember exactly when I had heard it, but apparently one of my husband's customers had recently ended his own life after his company had gone bankrupt. The word *tosan* referred to the exorbitant interest rates charged by black-market money lenders, thirty per cent in ten days, while *tōsan* could be read as either *father* or *bankruptcy*. Still, I wasn't a particularly talented poet either, and the short ditty – implying that my husband was responsible for the man's death – relied on a fairly mediocre pun, and I doubted that you could even call it a real haiku.

I could see the proprietress's lips twitching as the two of us continued to play around with the empty bottle of Yamazaki. Things progressed quickly after this drinking get-together, and a month later, I got divorced. I broke up with the high school teacher shortly afterward because I didn't like having to get horribly drunk whenever I met him, and those assignments, full of songs like 'North Airport' and 'The Yoke of Love', were simply too demanding on me. But for some reason, even after the divorce, I still turned to my ex-husband whenever I found myself in trouble, availing myself of his help time and time again.

I know that I keep swinging back and forth between topics, that this all began with a statement given by a sixty-something woman who hated working as an in-store food sample dealer, prompting me to visit a certain bar and enquire with the proprietress there about my husband's old flame, but I still have one more juicy extra.

Essentially, according to the proprietress, my husband, visiting the establishment alone one night and drinking himself into a stupor, started prattling on about his past episodes with various women, when he happened to start talking about me.

'But your wife, she's a keeper, wouldn't you say?' the proprietress said. 'She's so slender and pretty.'

My husband let out a long, deep sigh. 'Pretty, huh?' He gulped down his remaining liquor. 'She… she ain't really with me 'cause she likes me, you know…? Well, I guess she *is* kinda cute, but she's so cold, like she doesn't have a shred of feminine charm.'

My husband's assessment of me came as a disappointment, as I had thought that we were one in the belief that relationships ought to be as simple and as straightforward as possible. Still, at least he didn't deny me my looks. Broadly speaking, I *was* sorry that I hadn't given him enough of an opportunity to confirm even a shred of my affection for him, but to put it bluntly, *unfriendly* was how most people thought of me, no matter where I went or what I did. The bar proprietress's relentless kindness in furnishing me with all this information without my even having had to probe for it was probably a tacit expression of agreement with that public perception. Or maybe it was just that she secretly had feelings of her own for my husband.

Of all the inexplicable mysteries that I have encountered in the world, the most vexing is this phenomenon that results in me clamming up, unable to respond to a conversation partner who will in turn fly off the handle. Whether they're a business partner or a lover, whenever I'm alone with someone, they inevitably end up saying something like 'Hey, are you even listening? What have I done to piss you off now?'

No, it isn't at all uncommon. I'm willing to admit that I often neglect to respond when someone addresses me, that at times I fail to even notice them. Moreover, my lack of any real grasp of the *necessity* of responding may well have been the headstream of this great river, and it's simply undeniable that my relationships with men my own age tend to last only from one full moon to the next. I know this to be a direct consequence of the fact that I had spent much of my early formative years with someone to whom there had been no need to respond at all, but I honestly don't see it as any great vice. For that matter, the definition of the word *vice* is by no means straightforward. For example, shortly after my divorce, I heard a wild rumour that one of my ex-husband's clients in the investment world had been arrested, the charge being that the man, a monk, had sealed the bodily remains of his deceased mistress inside the Kannon Bodhisattva statue in the main hall of his temple and had then made heartfelt offerings toward her for the next five years.

'Stop lingering! Keep moving!' came a roar from the milling crowd.

With the level of obstruction that it was causing to traffic, the police officer, swinging his bamboo baton, longer than he was tall, began to disperse the crowd on the bridge.

At any rate, all the television stations in Tamil Nadu had been broadcasting news footage of the Adyar incessantly since early morning. I couldn't fathom how they had managed to do it, but they had set up a stepladder in the middle of this chaos, all but erecting a small tower atop which perched a man with a television camera on his shoulder filming the roiling river and the myriad onlookers from above. A group of children were jumping up and down, making the Indian peace sign to the camera. Watching that live television broadcast, viewers felt a vague stirring in their hearts, and ran blindly out from their houses to the bridge, where they placed their hands on the railing to stare out across the river.

'What do you think you're doing? Hey, get a move on! Quit dawdling!' echoed the cries of the police officer.

It's always best not to disobey Indian police officers. When I asked Ganesha in my Japanese class the other day why his front tooth was chipped, he replied that it had been broken when he accidentally tried to enter a women-only train carriage as a student and was knocked to the ground by the policewoman guarding the entrance.

Devaraj aside, when I looked on the peaceful faces of my students, I found it difficult to believe that they could have grown up in such a violent environment, and I suspected the anecdotes that occasionally filled the room were no more than idle stories.

When I first looked over the student roster that I had received from the human resources department upon my arrival in India, I couldn't help but notice that most of the names – Vishnu, Shiva, Ganesha, and so forth – were related to gods in one way or another. At the time, such choice of name struck me as somehow irreverent, but I later learned during the course of my daily classes that these were simply common Hindu names – like Tarō or Ichirō in Japan – and my sense of awe quickly dissipated. To be honest, a significant portion of my classes was always given over to chitchat in a mix of Tamil, English, and Japanese, and while I would like to say that such open-ended conversation was essential to help them get used to the Japanese language, this was really just the result of my lack of control over the classroom and the students' lack of respect for me as their teacher.

For example, one day just before the end of the morning test in which I had instructed the students to recite the vocabulary and sentence patterns that I had taught the day before, Ananda, sitting directly in front of me, said in a cheerful tone of voice, 'Sensei! Did you see *Let's Speak Japanese!* on YouTube?'

I began to explain that he couldn't just say *did you see*, that he had to use the perfective form *have you seen*, but Shiva gave me no time to launch into a proper grammatical breakdown, crying out almost menacingly, 'I saw, I saw! Konomi-chan in *Let's Speak Japanese!* She's cute!'

My students were supposed to be computer programmers from Hindu Technologies, one of the most prestigious companies in all of Tamil Nadu. According to Mr Karthikeyan, the IT industry has a five-level international standard called Capability Maturity Model Integration, or CMMI, used to evaluate the reliability of companies. Apparently, the first company in the world to achieve the highest score was an Indian one based in Bangalore, while most other organisations that had achieved a Level 5 score to date were likewise based in India. 'Our goal is to achieve Level 5 ourselves,' the vice president said to me once with laboured breath, remarking also that the recruitment of Japanese instructors to develop the company's human resources was part of this broader effort. At any rate, Hindu Technologies was now a CMMI Level 4 business, and my students were supposed to be part of an elite group having cleared more than a dozen hurdles to reach their present positions – which made it all the more incredible to see how they managed to unearth so many inane nothings from across the internet. It seemed that a great many Japanese language schools had hit on a winning marketing strategy for the recruitment of prospective students – those foreigners with a latent ambition to one day see Japan for themselves – employing a pretty girl with a twinkle in her eye for the express purpose of luring them in. The sparkling gazes of my students spoke to the success of such publicity campaigns. I had no idea just how many such programs there were, but no sooner was Konomi-chan's name said aloud than the room was thrown into an almighty commotion.

'No! No! Ayano-chan from *Speaking Japanese* is cute!' Ganesha exclaimed, when –

'No! Airin-chan from *I Love Japanese* is cuter!' Muruganantham shouted even louder.

Just as this fresh battle was about to turn ugly, Devaraj silenced the class with an audible *Shhh!* and raised his index finger into the air to get everyone's attention. 'Yurika-chan from *All Together in Japanese* is the cutest of them all,' he proclaimed.

As was to be expected of the king of the classroom, he put the situation in order to a round of applause. But perhaps it was a different matter when it came to girls, as just when I thought the matter settled, Shiva turned up the heat once more. 'No, you're wrong. Konomi-chan is the best!'

In the end, the debate had circled back to its starting point, but Shiva had corrected his grammar, even using a superlative sentence pattern before continuing. 'I want to meet Konomi-chan! I'll go to Japan next year!'

Ignoring Shiva, his nose flaring as he continued to ramble on, I said, 'Do you remember, everyone? What sentence pattern do we use when we want to *invite* someone?'

'We ask a question with a negative polite verb, like when you say in English *won't you*,' Devaraj answered without a moment's delay.

'That's right,' I answered. 'Shiva-san, please use that sentence structure to invite Konomi-chan.'

As I turned back to him, Shiva broke into a dauntless grin. 'Konomi-san,' he said, 'won't you come to a hotel with me?'

Ah, I thought. In India, *going to a hotel* meant going out to eat. I could only imagine the destructive potential of this statement if by chance any of my students should have an opportunity to ask a Japanese woman out, but explaining the difference in meaning would take too much effort, so I pretended not to have heard him.

Next, Vishnu's lips curled in a wide smile. 'Sensei! My brother went to McDonald's in Kawasaki, and now she works there.'

I had heard several times that this older brother – a star employee at a world-famous CMMI Level 5 company called Bangalore Brilliant Technologies, rated higher even than our own Hindu Technologies – had been working in Kanagawa for the past three years. As far as Vishnu was concerned, his brother was practically an Olympic gold medallist, having graduated at the top of his class from the Faculty of Engineering at his university. Indeed, Vishnu was always showing me a photograph of his brother and his wife laughing in front of the Gundam statue at Odaiba in Tokyo as they pushed around a baby stroller. His eyes were positively aglow as in stilted Japanese he tried to explain his ambition to follow in his brother's footsteps, but none of it made any sense.

'*Makudo*?' I repeated. 'Your brother works at a *Makudo* in Kawasaki? Why?' Noticing that everyone was staring back at me blankly, I continued. 'In Japan, people call McDonald's *Makudo*. Everyone, repeat after me: *Makudo*.' Caught up in the moment, I had begun to introduce new vocabulary, when it struck me that this reaction was perhaps somewhat unfair to the students.

From what I had heard, those employees at Indian companies who were transferred to Japan were highly privileged in terms of salary and benefits, and I just couldn't imagine Vishnu's vaunted brother asking a customer *Would you like fries with that?*

Patiently I repeated the question once more, when finally Vishnu's face lit up with realisation. 'Ah! Not my *brother*! My *sister*! My sister, my brother's wife!'

It turned out that he had misspoken, that he had meant his sister-in-law when it had sounded as if he was talking about his brother. In any event, with the question of whether it was really okay for a Hindu to engage in the sale of beef burgers still nagging at me, I decided to schedule an unannounced vocabulary test on kinship terms for family members and relatives the following Friday. Despite their grand names, Shiva and Vishnu and the others continued with their inane banter, so mundane and childish that my mouth slammed shut in confusion whenever I thought so much as to nod my head in feigned understanding, let alone try to get a word in edgewise. Every now and then, however, their banter would lead to discoveries that proved deeply insightful.

For example, the conversation turned at one point to a page in the textbook describing a German lady experiencing the Japanese tea ceremony for the first time. The book included a word that the students hadn't yet learned, *seiza*, describing it only as *a traditional way of sitting*, so I was left with no choice but to demonstrate by kneeling formally atop my own chair, folding my legs beneath my thighs and resting my buttocks on my heels as I explained, 'This is Japanese *seiza*.'

'Is it a punishment?' the students responded.

I rushed to clarify that no, no, it wasn't, that this was just how Japanese people normally sat in formal situations, when the conversation took yet another turn, shifting to the types of corporal punishment used by teachers in Indian schools.

Shiva, who was convinced that Konomi-chan would meet him at Narita Airport if he could only travel to Japan, told me that a former teacher of his had made him stand atop his chair until the end of class, holding his hands up in the air the whole time while the rest of his classmates laughed at him. As far as I was concerned, what he described was halfway to being psychological abuse. Then Vishnu, whose sister-in-law was working diligently in a red McDonald's uniform in Kawasaki, told me about a punishment called *kneeling*. As he described it, this insane punishment involved balancing on your knees with your hands behind your back grasping your ankles, and what was worse, walking around the school building several times atop scalding sand. But apparently, that was just the beginning. The corporal punishments handed out by teachers had, it seemed, been particularly severe at the middle school level, but following a certain widely publicised suicide at one school, were recently banned altogether.

Even so, as these two individuals finished recounting their tales of corporal punishment, the other students, who looked to have been trying desperately to keep from interrupting, quickly joined in, taking turns to clap one another not on the back, but on the shoulder, erupting with a vigour that was clearly beyond what would have been socially acceptable in Japan. As I laid eyes on their innocent, unaffected smiles, I realised that it would be completely useless to try to get through to them by attempting to feign a harsh or intimidating attitude.

All the same, there were a great many occasions when I was reminded that, for better or for worse, my students were honest people, born and raised in a country where there was nothing to be gained by speaking up.

As I explained the sentence pattern used to express one's own wants, I struck on a fresh idea, asking, 'If you could be reincarnated, what would you like to be in your next life?'

Of course it was necessary for me to explain the words *raise*, meaning *next life*, and *umarekawarimasu*, meaning *reborn*, neither of which was included in the elementary level textbook, but I couldn't help being startled when they all answered along the same lines.

'I want to be reborn as my mother's son,' they said, or 'I want to be reborn as my father's son,' or 'I want to be reborn as my brother's brother.'

Without any hesitation whatsoever, my students' responses were unanimous.

One of them gave a rather convoluted rejoinder, and after more than ten minutes of trying to untangle his English-speckled Japanese, he answered, 'I want to be my father's father.'

He said that in the next life he wanted to give back to his parents the exact same gifts that they had given him.

On the whiteboard I wrote the word *ongaeshi*.

'The word *on* means *benefit*, and *kaeshi* means *to give back*. So *ongaeshi* means an act of returning a kindness that you received from someone else,' I said in dry explanation.

In short, Indian people loved their families, loved their lives, loved the present moment. From my students' remarks, I sensed deeply that their greatest desire was to remain as they were now, with their current selves, with their current families, forever and ever, in this life and the next.

There are a great many prejudices in this world, and one of them is no doubt the idea that Indians are a deeply religious people with transcendent thoughts that stretch beyond this life. For example, if I were to ask whether they believed in an afterlife, almost everyone in the class would raise their hands without even the slightest hesitation. But this question would be a trap. Speaking for myself, *religion* is a vague, mystical concept that touches on a realm beyond this reality, but for Indian people it incorporates ideas rooted in this world such as the cycle of samsara and reincarnation.

In any case, my students' undying love for their families and their present lives left me in a state of awe. At that point I realised that Devaraj, most surprisingly given his usual disruptive conduct, hadn't looked up once during this entire exchange, responding when I repeated the question only with the words 'I don't know'.

As I approached, I found him engaged in drawing an image in his notebook of a woman with a forlorn look on her face, her long hair parted in the middle of her forehead.

'Get out of this classroom right now. I'll be marking you as absent today,' I ordered sternly.

'I'm sorry,' he answered, the apology sounding from his lips so rare that my own mouth slammed firmly shut.

Just as I tried mustering the strength to complain a little more forcefully, he suddenly continued, as he always did when saying something mysterious, 'My father wasn't home. My mother was born a child.'

'What do you mean?' I prompted.

'How do you say *give birth* in Japanese?' he asked, falling back on English.

'*Umimasu*,' I answered.

'My father wasn't home,' Devaraj continued, 'but

my mother gave birth.' Then he added the following explanation, as though of little import, 'For a year, my father left the country. He went on a trip with me.'

It took me a moment to fully grasp what he was saying, as he had mispronounced the word *ryokō*, meaning *trip* or *holiday*, as *ryōko*. Speakers of Tamil don't pay much heed to the length of vowels, so this kind of error wasn't particularly uncommon. As my lips moved to correct his pronunciation, my hand turned almost automatically to the whiteboard.

My father was out of the country for a year, but my mother gave birth to a child, I wrote.

It wasn't all that long since I had taught contrastive conjunctions modelled on the phrase *It was raining yesterday, but it is sunny today*, and at the very least, this could prove to be a useful opportunity for revision.

As if to conclude his story, Devaraj added, 'The child was *adopted* to another family.' Once more, he used the English term as a crutch.

In silence I wrote the word *yōshi* on the whiteboard next to *adopt*. 'You don't have to remember this one,' I murmured.

As usual, I was carrying a stack of seventy-eight A4-sized sheets of copy paper stapled together in my hand. I had been pressed into serving on this curry-scented long-range voyage to pay off my debts, and day in, day out, I had to repeat this pattern of formulating lesson plans, putting them into practice, then formulating more lesson plans. Charlatan language teacher as I was, somehow managing to get by with my makeshift materials, I flipped through my handwritten notes, which I had scribbled down with the help of a trusty reference book. Tempted though I am to say more, if I shall make any remarks here about *fate*, I will restrict myself to one event only – the festival that I will mention later – and nothing more. Anyway, at the time, I didn't want to hear why Devaraj had gone out of his way to bring up this fateful topic, nor why he and his father had been away from home for so long.

And so I issued the class fresh instructions. 'Alright, everyone, open your English textbooks and take a look at the vocabulary.'

As we began a new lesson, I had the students return to their English reference books and begin the process of reviewing, explaining and memorising the new vocabulary. One of the new words was *sumō*, which I introduced as a type of Japanese wrestling, a popular traditional sport, gesturing to an illustration from the textbook.

'Sensei. Is it okay to say someone *does sumō*?' Devaraj asked.

'It will do,' I answered. 'But it's more common to say someone is a *sumō* wrestler.'

Nonetheless, Devaraj, bad loser that he was, continued, 'My father did *sumō* every day.'

I had never heard of any Indian *sumō* wrestlers, but I decided to let that slide for a moment in order to address the low-hanging fruit. 'In Japanese, there are two words for father. When you're talking about your own, you say *chichi*; when you're talking about someone else's, you say *otōsan*. Think of it as similar to the difference between *dad* and *father*,' I cautioned, before asking, 'What do you mean, he did *sumō* every day? Who did he compete against? Where?'

'My dad did *sumō* with a bear in my village,' Devaraj replied immediately.

'A bear…? In your village…?'

I had already introduced the Japanese word for *bear* – *kuma* – along with the names of other major animals such as cats, dogs, cows, goats, sheep, tigers, elephants and so forth, but in the time that it took me to think of a response, Devaraj had already started speaking loudly in Tamil with the students around him, the classroom descending into a state of chaos. Over the next ten minutes, with the help of another student's translation, he explained in a mix of English and Japanese that his father was an entertainer who toured the local villages showing off his wrestling skills by grappling with specially-trained bears. Devaraj, it seemed, had been responsible for collecting the coins given by onlookers. That must have been what he meant when he said that he and his father were off travelling for a year.

At that moment, I could see in my mind's eye a young Devaraj clutching a bowl and collecting the coins scattered around the ring, moving from person to person and asking for money with an adorable smile on his face. Faced with that wry, puckered grin, the marker pen in my right hand slid quickly across the whiteboard.

My father used to wrestle with bears I wrote, before turning back to the students. 'We've studied this several times already, and it's used in a variety of situations, but who can tell me the function of the habitual verb *used to* here? Yes, Ananda?' I asked, gesturing toward him.

'It means when someone did a profession,' he answered.

'That's right.' I nodded. 'Devaraj's father was a *sumō* wrestler by profession. He isn't any longer though, so we need to use the past habitual here.' I paused there, before asking the students to repeat the phrase *My father used to wrestle with bears* three times.

I had already introduced this exceptionally common grammatical pattern some time ago, but this example sentence, having arisen entirely by chance, was the perfect opportunity for some spur-of-the-moment revision.

But that wasn't all.

A little while later, after I had finished introducing the main auxiliary verbs expressing the acts of giving and receiving, Devaraj raised his hand once more. 'Sensei. How do you say *bowl* in Japanese?'

'*Owan*,' I answered.

No sooner did I close my mouth than Devaraj began to recount another episode about his father. 'My father did *sumō* with bears every day. The customers gave money to my bowl.'

'The customers *put money in* your bowl,' I corrected him. 'The customers aren't *giving* money to the bowl, they are *putting* the money inside it.'

Devaraj nodded. 'Sensei. Is this okay? The man gave the Buddha a *guyo*.'

'*Guyo*?' I stared back, but Devaraj fell unusually silent.

On the topic of the Buddha –

'Everyone, who can tell me what religion people in Japan follow?'

'Buddhism,' the students answered in English.

'In Japanese, Buddhism is called *bukkyō*. Repeat after me: *bukkyō*.'

'*Bukkyō*.'

'And where is the founder of Buddhism from?' I asked.

'China,' they answered as though by rote.

In order to give them some basic knowledge of Japanese culture, I launched into a brief explanation of Buddhism and introduced them to some related vocabulary, starting with the word that had come up a moment earlier, *Hotoke-sama*, meaning *Buddha*.

In any event, as was becoming my habit, I shelved Devaraj's strange remark for now, and without explaining the various meanings of the term *Hotoke-sama*, turned to the whiteboard to launch into further explanation of the verbs of giving and receiving, all the while wondering to myself whether he hadn't perhaps meant to say the word *kuyō*, meaning *offering*. Nonetheless, I dismissed the idea without a second thought. After all, he couldn't possibly know such a difficult Japanese word that *I* certainly hadn't taught him. Instead, I wrote the sentence from earlier – *The customers put money in my bowl* – up on the whiteboard and asked everyone to repeat it out loud.

Each student spoke the sentence one by one, and when finally it was Devaraj's turn, a stray thought occurred to me as I watched his nonchalant expression.

A worm of an idea had crossed my mind, a nagging

suspicion that Devaraj might in fact have been purposefully trying to prompt me to come up with helpful example sentences by suggesting the best topics for us to review new grammatical patterns. Earlier, when he had said *The customers put money in my bowl*, I finally realised that there was something deliberate about his choice of topic, almost as if he was intentionally encouraging me to correct his mistakes. If so, then he wasn't only playing a knowing role in making up for my amateur teaching by demonstrating the purpose of each lesson to the rest of the class, but he was also guiding me through various contrived situations to more strongly impress on the other students the grammatical point in question. Could it be that in large part, the lessons were proceeding smoothly precisely because of his intercessions?

Perhaps this very situation could be summed up using the sentence structure that I was currently teaching, something like *Devaraj-san offers me help* or *I received Devaraj-san's help*? But I would be damned if I was going to write those example phrases on the whiteboard.

Anyway, their mental ages aside, my students had all graduated from top universities and had all been immediately hired as computer programmers at Hindu Technologies, the famous CMMI Level 4-rated IT company based in Tamil Nadu. At the same time, it seemed to be the case that Devaraj alone had endured uniquely painful experiences that set him apart from his classmates. He had no siblings other than the child who was adopted out to another family, and he had lost his parents one after the other. Someone would later tell me that he was nonetheless an unusually bright child, and that an influential figure in his home village had therefore helped pay for his schooling all the way through to university.

The sound of the tall police officer with his chubby posterior moving back and forth pounding the railing of the bridge with his long bamboo baton grew louder and louder.

Beneath the bridge, the waters were raging furiously, while a huge crowd had gathered to watch on from above. Though I had no evidence to back me up, I was convinced that these faces had no doubt walked this same path a hundred years earlier, had come then as they were now to watch this river that, once every century, hummed its way through all of mankind's creations before arduously beginning the cycle afresh. No matter how the onlookers were threatened or coaxed, they refused to budge. After a couple more rounds, the police officer, probably having finally grown tired of the ever-increasing number of rubber-necking bystanders, suddenly let out a strange cry, striking out with his knee at the mass of people swarming in front of him. To his side, a family of five each wearing matching black Batman T-shirts held up their smartphones and took smiling selfies, while an old man on a bicycle with a sack of green bananas hanging behind him slipped between the cars and motorbikes, humming a tune as he weaved his way through the traffic jam. In the sky above those unripe bananas, a distant cloud hovered.

I remembered it clearly, stepping out from my

apartment just a short while ago for the first time in three days, walking through the rubble and the mud and the garbage. I had flinched at the smell of ruin that hung in the air, but at the same time, I was strangely moved when I found trash that had obviously been discarded after the flood had finished ploughing through the city, such as a fresh banana peel or a paper cup that someone must have just used for tea. Even at a time like this, human beings still had the power to add fresh rubbish to the earth. The soothing raindrops streaking down that brand new garbage reflected the sky, the clouds, the morning sun of a brand new Chennai. And it wasn't only the trash that had returned – all the noise and the exhaust fumes that had permeated the city before the flood had been reinstated as well. Within a few hours of the waters receding, the city had been brought back up to boiling point and was spilling over anew.

In that deep blue sky, I spotted an airborne figure sliding past the edge of the clouds, his wings scattering the light. To his right, another flyer with a smartphone in hand – apparently equipped with the latest model of aerial wings complete with an automated braking function that could be used one-handed – coursed through the sky without so much as glancing ahead. Once he passed in front of the first flyer, he made an abrupt left turn without any directional gestures, narrowly avoiding a collision, and the two just barely passed one another by. The first flyer, the one who had been placed in danger by the other, violently extended one hand in a gesture of protest, but the erratic flyer continued to glide away without even once taking his eyes from his phone.

On the ground, people were still managing to avoid the police officer cursing at the top of his voice, clapping their hands and hooting at each other as they crowded together. A group of young people were busy taking selfies as they flailed their arms and legs, looking for all the world as if they were about to fall head over heel into the river.

There was a crew-cut trio with strong physiques, one of whom slapped the first of his companions on the back as he let out an explosive gale of laughter and exclaimed, 'Look at you, you're about to fall, you dumbass!'

The target of his friend's derision quickly puffed up his cheeks and held out his hands, feigning anger. 'Dumbass? Dumbass? Who's the dumbass? Who do you think you are, talking to me like that? Gimme a break already.'

With an especially pronounced theatrical gesture, the instigator looked up at the sky. 'You saw him, right? He just passed by. That was my uncle, and he's got a flight licence that can shut up any wailing kid.'

'What happened to your old man, anyway?'

'Come on, flight privileges were restricted to one individual among relatives to the third degree of kinship. You mustn't be all that close if you don't know that.'

'Didn't your uncle go to jail last year for taking bribes, though?'

'How stupid are you? How else are you supposed to get ahead in the world?'

With this, the one who had started the argument rolled up the right sleeve of his T-shirt and flexed his muscles. 'If you've got power, all you've got to say is *please*, and people will start greasing your palm.' With one hand raised high into the air, he looked out at the flying passers-by flitting across the sky in all directions.

'You ought to be able to make a career out of flying traffic,' his companion chuckled.

The man laughed. 'Yeah, sure. As if I could afford it. I saw a flying licence up for auction on the net yesterday, along with a two-wing set complete with collision mitigation brakes and auxiliary wings, and by this morning the highest bid was enough to buy two houses in Ashok Nagar. Tell you what, when I catch a break, I'll give you a house call from up there in the sky.'

'What do you mean a *house call*?'

'A man's gotta take a piss sometime.'

'You asshole!' With this, the second man quickly placed his hands under his partner's armpits and pushed him toward the handrail overlooking the river.

'Help me, O Adyar! Namaste!' cried the first. The three men broke out into joint laughter and took a few more selfies, the sound of digital camera shutters echoing one after the next.

As the men romped around, I looked between their figures down at the surface of the water, rough and hidden from view. For the past hundred years, this unfathomable muddy stream with its incessant howl had never been so close to the people of Chennai than it was now, nor had it been paid such ardent attention. When first I arrived in Chennai, the Adyar had been relatively low-lying, and everyone would simply pinch their noses as they walked quickly past it. But once, on my way to work, I saw an extraordinary sight, a person wading across its surface with overhand strokes as the water constantly rippled with methane gas rising up from its depths.

On the bridge, still alive with cheerful Tamil chatter, Devaraj, with an unenthused look, thrust his rake into the hundred-year-old mud and ploughed it back, his shapely, slender legs moving back and forth with each languid motion. After several long draws, there was an audible chink as his rake collided again with something new.

Slowly he approached the sidewalk occupied by the selfie trio until just a moment earlier and retrieved from the mud what looked like a small, faded, old-fashioned glass case.

Even before I could draw close, a light switched on in the back of my head. I could barely make out a vague silhouette through the muddy glass, but I already recognised the figure that I had seen once during a visit to a temple while on an elementary school field trip.

I remembered back to a time in fifth grade when my teacher had led the whole class on a bus trip to a small seaside temple. The elderly priest, his pronunciation difficult to follow probably on account of ill-fitting dentures, gave a long talk peppered with terms and phrases like *potalaka* and *saints who crossed the sea* and *leading the masses on the path of enlightenment* and thereafter led us to an old glass case in a corner of the hall opposite the enshrined main image. We were enthralled at once by the sight of its contents.

'It's a mummified mermaid,' the priest said, before turning to face the glass case as he put his hands together in prayer.

The mummy was a rarity in Japan, with what looked like both a human leg and a fish fin protruding from its body. According to the priest, little was known about the figure other than that it had been donated to the temple at some point during the Edo period.

Needless to say, it wasn't the priest's long lecture on those monks who had forsaken their past lives at the sea's edge that occupied the class's attention afterwards, but rather the mummified mermaid. The tale went through countless variations as it was reworked from one recitation to the next, but it finally developed into the following version as told by my classmate Okamura, 'My mum says there used to be a beach around these parts a long time ago. She said one day a mermaid washed up on the shore, but everyone bullied her to death. So ever since, this place has been cursed by the mermaid's angry spirit.'

Okamura had recently joined our class after transferring to our school from Osaka, and since the very moment of his arrival he had busied himself winning the hearts and minds of his classmates with his storytelling ability and enterprising attitude. He claimed to hate Putchin pudding, so on the morning of the day when it was supposed to included on the lunchtime menu at school, all those classmates who wanted to be better friends with him lined up outside his house. Okamura was born and raised in Osaka, but moved with his mother to her parents' hometown when his folks got divorced. That was why his mother was such a repository of knowledge when it came to the local area.

After the previous comment Okamura continued in a hushed voice, 'At this school, they say there's a mermaid in every class.'

In short, this was just an excuse to force people to pull down their underwear in front of others, even though no one had ever been demonstrated to be a mermaid by this kind of physical examination.

I understood this well because my mother was a mermaid. She never said as much, but I knew. Of all my classmates, I was the only one who understood that real mermaids don't speak. The fact that no one else had recognised this as one of a mermaid's fundamental traits ought to have been sufficient proof that they knew nothing whatsoever about the topic. The fairy tale *The Little Mermaid* even mentions it at one point. I was so concerned that someone might inadvertently stumble upon this truth that one day after school, I hid the library's copy of the tale under my school uniform and whisked it off home – an extreme measure that I still believe was entirely necessary.

Ever since I was a child, I had hardly ever heard my mother speak. When she was forced to say something while out and about, she would stare down at her feet and whisper in the softest of voices, and as soon as someone asked her to repeat herself, she would disappear like a mermaid thrown back into the water. But those occasions were few and far between. When she went shopping, she would make do by pointing toward whatever she wanted, and since my earliest memories, I had always been by her side, ready to direct a confused store clerk whenever necessary by saying, 'That one, please.'

As I mentioned earlier, my stepfather had already been married before. From what I gathered, his ex-wife seemed to be a particularly outspoken woman, the kind who prattled on incessantly every hour of the day, and if you failed to respond to her quickly enough, she would grumble in complaint before moving immediately on to something else. She criticised her husband for not being around on weekends and holidays, grumbled about his salary, and found fault with his mother when she dropped by to visit and criticized her when she didn't, until by the end of their marriage, she cursed him for literally everything and anything, from the way that he ate, to the way that he pulled the string on the electric lamps, to the fact that the only restaurant that he had taken her to before tying the knot was a cheap tavern, even to the water fixtures in the kitchen, the aluminium windows frames, the surface of the tatami mats, and the stains on the ceiling before finally declaring that she had fallen in love with another man with whom she promptly eloped.

Six months later, upon being introduced to my mother, my father took an instant liking to her. My mother was radiant and beautiful, and she didn't utter so much as a word. They say that a married man and woman don't have to offer one another bouquets of roses every day in order to show their love, that it's a blessing in disguise when a man doesn't have to listen to a beautiful wife complain and curse. My father loved drinking and had no need for conversation so long as he could enjoy a simple snack, so no problems arose between them.

It must have been right after our social studies field trip to the temple, but one day as I was walking with my mother down the shopping street, we ran into one of my classmates in front of the butcher's shop. Entering the store, my mother pointed to this and that as usual and I interpreted for her by reading the finger gestures by which she specified the quantities. 'Excuse me, can we have two hundred grams of ground pork, please?' I asked the shopkeeper while my mother watched on closely. When she brought out her purse to pay, my classmate put her mouth up to my ear. 'Your mother is so pretty, Yotchan, but she kind of looks like a *yukimba*.' Having whispered those words, my classmate ran off before I could fully process what she had said.

A *yukimba*, or snow hag. She was referring to the protagonist of a picture book by the same name, one of the most popular titles on the shelves of the class library in the corner of the classroom and a tale that could probably be likened to *The Snow Woman* in the national constituency. To be honest, I had no idea who had added the book to the class collection or when, but its popularity with my classmates was entirely based on the illustrations contained within its covers – in other words, the quiet power of the dreaded *yukimba* to instantly freeze the hearts of all those who laid eyes on her. On one occasion a boy who had been engrossed reading the book during recess had to be taken to the nurse's office after peeing his pants at the mere mention of the word *snow* later in the day, but that didn't stop him from opening its pages again the very next morning. Such was the mysterious power that the book held over us. Our classmate must have been referring to the fact that my mother was extremely pale of complexion, moved at an unusually slow pace, said nothing, and wore no expression to speak of. My mother's nature, however, had never inconvenienced me in any way. When I was feeling low or downbeat, I would sneak up behind her as she knitted, and we would spend an eternity pushing one another back-to-back. My mother loved to knit and sew, and she was masterful in the kitchen too. I never met any of my maternal grandparents or relatives, so my mother's life history remains unclear to me even today, but I heard that she grew up by the sea, that her own birth mother passed away shortly after she was born, and that she hadn't got along well with her stepmother.

In spring we used to pick mugwort together on the embankment by the river. We walked together staring out over the water. Whenever my mother saw a familiar face she would wave to them in polite greeting. Of course, this was so that she could avoid having to say hello in person. I watched as mother ducks and their young ducklings bobbed along the surface and white egrets craned their necks in the middle of the river. As we walked, my footprints sank into the moist soil along the riverbank. My mother often turned round to glance back at her own footprints, a vaguely childish expression falling over her face. She seemed to enjoy the fact that when she trod upon the soil, the ground took it in stride, altering its form to accommodate her every footstep.

When we got home, we made mugwort rice dumplings. I did my best to imitate the movements of my mother's hands. After carefully washing away any dirt, we tore off the mugwort leaves and boiled them with baking soda. I was in charge of pounding the leaves in a mortar. My mother kneaded them with sugar, tore them into pieces, placed them inside the steamer, and covered the lid. Fifteen minutes later, she positioned herself in front of the steamer once more while I waited by her side. The moment that she removed the lid, I inhaled deeply that wonderful aroma, and my mother's cheeks, always so expressionless, loosened slightly.

I was an idle daydreamer as a child. For example, on Sundays I would be sitting at home, my mother knitting by my side, and I would suddenly think to myself *Ah, today's Sunday*. Then the thought would come to me that there must be another Sunday off somewhere else. There would be *my* Sunday, and then that other Sunday too. They were both Sundays, and there was never any question of only one of them being real or right. And in that case, I mused, there must be other Mondays and Tuesdays too. I thought about those Wednesdays that weren't mine, the Thursdays that could have been. I wondered about alleys that I hadn't walked, landscapes that I hadn't seen, songs that I hadn't heard. I closed my eyes. Words that my mother hadn't spoken. My mother's voice, which I hadn't heard. They would blow as the wind of another Friday, another Saturday, somewhere, elsewhere. Or they would fall as the rain on another Sunday. As my mother and I pushed each other gently back and forth, I imagined her words and voice dripping onto the petals of cosmos flowers and the leaves of starworts, splashing on tin roofs, running down gutters, glittering in street drains, flowing through culverts into rivers and finally emptying into the open sea.

My mother shied away from every opportunity to be involved as a parent in my school life. Whenever my teacher distributed handouts that we were instructed to show to our mums and dads, notices informing them of class visits, parent-teacher conferences, home calls, field days, and so forth, she would silently shake her head. I offered my homeroom teacher every conceivable excuse that I could bring to mind. 'She has a cold,' I might say, or 'She had an epileptic seizure this morning,' or 'She's on a self-improvement training trip,' to the extent that he began to doubt my mother's very existence.

One day my homeroom teacher even dropped by in person and spent fifteen minutes kneeling formally on a cushion as he lectured my mother about my performance at school. 'She's a serious kid, but she doesn't raise her hand very often in class, and she doesn't come across as very assertive. She doesn't seem to have any close friends, and when everyone else is off playing during recess and lunch…'

My homeroom teacher left after discussing his findings alone with my mother, who simply nodded her chin up and down slowly with no expression on her face. In his report submitted to the coordinator of my year level, he wrote only, 'Student's parents gave their approval and consent for my instruction.' Once he was gone, I carefully swept away the fifteen minutes of resignation that had come to rest on the cushion that my homeroom teacher had used and put it away in the closet.

In my third year of middle school, I met a classmate who didn't speak to anyone at all.

She was a petite girl, and her grades were around the middle of the class, but I had no right to criticise her on that count. Basketball was particularly popular at the time, and when another girl asked her if she wanted to play with the rest of us, her expressionless face turned bright red, continuing to glance diagonally at the ground without responding. When we came back at the end of recess drenched in sweat, she was still sitting in the exact same position, still staring diagonally at the floor.

I would always pay attention to the way that my classmates and teachers acted in the girl's presence. Their attitudes toward her, I thought, probably weren't all that different from what my mother must have experienced as a child.

And so I watched. During music class, for instance, I watched as she silently mouthed the words to our class ensemble. Once, when it was her turn to read during Japanese class, the teacher pointed to her and said, 'Now, read this aloud.' As she started reading, he would bellow, 'Louder! I can't hear you!' or 'Do you think this is a game?' or 'Are you kidding me? You're doing this on purpose, aren't you? No one is going home today until you read it properly!' I watched him scold her seemingly forever, watched as my fellow classmates breathed exasperated sighs, watched as she hung her head by the window with cherry blossoms scattering in the wind behind her.

During recess, I would pretend to be reading a book or staring at the goldfish in its bowl in the corner of the room, but all the while I would be secretly watching her. In truth, I wasn't particularly friendly toward her, nor was she particularly friendly with me. Nonetheless, once on the way back to the classroom after a movie screening in the auditorium, she appeared by my side, turned my way, and looked for all the world as if about to say something in the smallest, most inaudible of voices.

The other girls in the class erupted in an uproar.

'Whoa, did you see that? Shindō just spoke!'

'Hey, did you hear that? Shindō spoke, everyone!'

They gathered around her, harassing her nonstop. 'Hey, hey, hey, say something again, say something, Shindō!'

As she made her way down the staircase alone, I thought to myself that she would never talk to me again.

At my middle school, we held class elections twice a year for the positions of class president and vice president.

During second semester, the former representative, acting as moderator, asked, 'Are there any candidates? Or if anyone wants to nominate someone, please raise your hand.'

After a few moments of silence in the sweltering room, a girl, one of the most popular in the class, languidly did just that. 'I nominate Shindō for class president and Nogawa for vice president!'

With those words, this girl, with whom I had never had any meaningful interaction, suggested my name for vice president. From her coy smirk, it was clear that she was trying to make a point. When I turned to look at the girl who had been nominated as class president, what I laid eyes on was the same black silhouette staring out the window as the summer clouds rolled in.

'You don't talk much, huh?' my classmates occasionally said to me.

Naturally. For me, there was very little difference to be found between words and silence. I usually responded to questions with a simple 'Yeah' or 'Right', especially when it came to the kinds of conversations that generally took place between girls. I wasn't used to overreacting like others so often did, exclaiming 'Huuuhhh?' or 'Seriously? Seriously? Hey, hey, seriously?' Now, however, having been nominated as one of our two class representatives, I knew for a fact that they regarded us as birds of a feather.

There were no further candidates after the moderator wrote our nominations on the blackboard, and with a tense atmosphere having fallen over everyone, the homeroom teacher, until that moment watching on from a corner, approached the front of the room and quietly erased our names.

Which brings me to a field trip that we went on during late autumn the same year.

The whole class was walking along a sandy beach while the girl and I trailed at the end of the procession. The long coastline curved gently around us. The other students were busy shouting and splashing each other in the waves, and our teacher was preoccupied scolding them. I kept quiet, staring at the fine sand, until before

I knew it, I found myself walking to the girl's right. The gentle, silent pressure from the people around us was reflected in the pace of the scene. Like the girl, I didn't talk to anyone else in the class.

A month earlier, my mother passed away from blood loss caused by uterine fibroids. I had gone to a friend's house for the first time in seemingly forever to borrow a manga comic that I had been wanting to read, and my father was out working late. She died without ever regaining consciousness. All at once, a scream like a vibrating bowstring rose over the rumbling of the sea as a girl, soaked by a huge wave breaking in front of her, cried out, my other classmates jeering and clapping their hands in amusement. The beach stretched as far as the eye could see, and the sand in front of my companion and me – both of us walking in stony silence behind our classmates – was covered in footprints, making it all the more difficult to leave our own trails. Nonetheless, we waited for the waves to stretch out their supple palms and clear away the tracks before us, and when we left our own trails, I felt my heart light up just a little to see them embraced by the roar of the rolling tides.

At that moment, I thought for a second that the whisper of a murmured word had just reached my ear. I lifted my face. Looking to my left, the girl continued to walk alongside me with her gaze downturned, but being taller than she was, I couldn't make out whether her lips had actually moved. Never having properly heard her voice before, I couldn't fully believe that the sound had truly risen up from her throat, and I wondered whether I hadn't instead discerned simply the singing of the waves in the growing twilight. The message of the waves was much smaller and fainter than any sound flowing from this person whose voice was lost, its contents beating against my chest, quietly, softly.

This is what it said:

'My mother died when I was young, so I was raised by my stepmother. There was an old lady who lived alone in an apartment nearby, and I loved her so much that I used to go visit her all the time. She never asked me "Why are you always so quiet?" She didn't slap me on the cheek when I didn't answer her, and she never said "So you don't want to talk to me, then? Well, in that case, I won't make you any dinner." Even though I didn't say anything, she was always talking to me. I responded to her in my heart. She lived off a pension and money sent by a son who lived far away, while also working as a caretaker of the apartment building where she lived.

'Sometimes, we took a stroll along the beach together. We played with our bare feet on the sand. We walked on our heels, left sideways footprints, and turned our feet in alternate directions to left and right. I was so happy when the beach responded to the prints that we left in the sand that we lost track of time drawing all kinds of shapes together.

'In spring, we went to the riverside and picked mugwort together. We made mugwort rice cakes and ate them together. I was always hungry, and I had never eaten anything so delicious before. Once, she stopped by my house to share some mugwort rice cakes that she had made. My stepmum thanked her and took them, but as soon as the old lady left, her expression and voice changed, like she had taken off a mask, and she said, "This won't do… No, not at all…" With a laugh, she opened the container and showed me its contents, before letting out a sigh.

'"She's done it again," my stepmum said. "Just look at this. All those mugwort leaves and stems. How could she be so daft? Well, you can't eat them. They're foul. When you boil mugwort, you need to add baking soda, at least a teaspoon. And what's this? You have to mix it with flour and knead it well. Did she really use fresh flour here? You ought to use at least two hundred grams for this amount, and around a tablespoon of sugar…"

'As she went to throw the rice cakes into the rubbish bin, container and all, she mumbled the entire recipe under her breath. I was impressed that she, who had never before so much as cooked a single mugwort rice cake, seemed to know every single ingredient and step of the process.

'It wasn't until six months later that the old lady was found dead in her bedroom by another tenant in her apartment building. The last time that we walked together on the beach, I was wearing my new athletic shoes. Maybe she had a premonition, as that day, with more than a month to go, the old lady suddenly said to me, "Ah, yes, it's your birthday coming up, isn't it?" She bought me the pair of trainers that I had always wanted. I couldn't really ask my stepmum for anything. I put them on in the shoe store, and my heart danced with joy as I walked hand in hand with her to the beach, happily wiping the sand off my feet and leaving brand new footprints with my brand new trainers. The world simply accepted them, responding to me without reserve. I looked over my fresh footprints and walked back and forth. I saw the plump, round clouds hanging over the sea. I wanted to keep on walking with the old lady. But for some reason, my new trainers disappeared from the shoebox the next day, and I was back to my old shoes again.'

As the sea breeze ruffled my hair, I wondered if my mother's voice had sounded like this.

I remembered the feel of the fabric on my skin as we pushed against each other's backs through the long afternoons. My mother hated doctors and never went for regular checkups or gynaecological examinations, and even though her periods were unusually strong and painful, she never tried to find out the cause. Given her nature, I don't think that she would have been able to endure the barbarism of having to explain every single detail of her condition to a doctor in words. On the day that we laid her ashes to rest, I opened the pages of the book that I had stolen from the library of my elementary school. The Little Mermaid gave up her voice and took on human form. I didn't know what my mother had gained from that exchange. As I tidied out her room, I realised that the only legs that my one and only mother had had in this world were me, and so I resolved to inscribe that belief in my heart forevermore.

I mentioned earlier the reputation that I was to acquire in later years. In fact the mystery of that public perception only deepened each time that a man clicked his tongue at me, coming out with some remark like, 'Are you mute, woman? Why don't you say something? Talk about unfriendly.' This was especially the case when my ex-husband, in one of his bouts of drunkenness, blurted one of his even more esoteric comments, as when he once told a kind bar proprietress that I didn't have a shred of feminine charm. Regardless, as a general principle, if you're on a date with me, and you start calling another woman on your smartphone, our conversation will be over, and if you slap the butt of my jeans and say, 'Oh my god, you're so unfriendly!' I won't waste a second before rising to my feet, pocketing my mobile, and taking a hard right turn for the exit.

There are no words written on a man's back to explain what he might mean by *friendly* or *cute*, or perhaps those definitions had always just been written in a handwriting that I couldn't read, but I did perhaps have a tendency to be complacent with the life directly in front of me. I did have a habit of thinking of it as just one possible life, of musing that a stone thrown among the infinite possibilities of the universe had simply happened to make contact here and cause a nosebleed. Much more important to me were the words that were never spoken, the words that could have been. It was the silent time with my mother after I was born into this world, before the *why* finally found me, that would never return. Half of all the men whom I dated were considerably older than me. When a man is a decade or two your senior, he is generally more tolerant. An older man, a man of my own generation, another older man and so forth. This alternating pattern of companionship unfolded in general terms until I married the third older man on the spur of the moment, divorced him on account of the fourth and asked the fifth for a loan. And so I eventually found myself in India.

'What are your dreams for the future?' I once asked everyone in my Japanese class.

'I want a house by the sea and an Audi car.'

'I want to work for a company with a good salary.'

'I'll be an executive who flies to work.'

As the students all gave their answers, it was Devaraj's that stood out the most, 'I want to marry for love.'

As I corrected his pronunciation, I couldn't help but think of the manifold layers to his yearning for *love* or a *love marriage* when a memory flashed before my eyes.

'Alright. Does anyone here have someone they love?' I asked for a show of hands, yet no one in the class, all of them young men in their early twenties, offered a response. Not only did none of them currently have a girlfriend, but the vast majority had no experience whatsoever of love or romance.

In this case, it would be misleading to imagine the typical Indian movie. Rather, some remarks on the local schooling system would probably be helpful to understand my students' responses. In India, boys and girls are allowed to partake in normal conversations in elementary and middle school, but from high school on, this atmosphere disappears, and if a boy and a girl engage in conversation at school, they will in very short order be severely reprimanded. Even in coeducational universities, men and women aren't permitted to talk to one another – all seats in the lecture halls are divided into male and female sections, and there are even surveillance cameras installed to maintain this separation of the sexes.

Ganesha told the class how he once tried to get a pretty girl to remember his face in his school classroom. 'Hey, hey, can I see your notes?' he said, covering his mouth with his hand to hide his missing teeth, when someone immediately tapped him on the shoulder from behind. 'Not at school,' admonished the security guard.

But for the students before me now, the syntax of the invitation patterns introduced in class and their example sentences – constructions like *Won't you come to a hotel with me?* – were just as absurd as watching a Japanese language school's YouTube video and sighing after the mascot girl in centre stage. It was unmistakable – no matter where you turned in this classroom, all my students were virgins.

It may seem natural according to Hindu custom to eliminate as much as possible any interactions between men and women, but then no sooner does the enigma of why coeducational schools exist in the first place arise than it dissolves back into the vast darkness of India. To put it bluntly, given what I had learned, it felt somewhat strange to see male and female employees – cafeteria staff, cleaning staff, and so on – talking and laughing with each other so naturally within the walls of Hindu Technologies. I had taken public buses on several occasions during my time here, and I distinctly remembered the passengers sitting apart as though to do so was simply a matter of course, with the men on the right side of the aisle and the women on the left.

'Everyone. Would you rather have an arranged marriage or marry for love?' I asked the class.

With the sole exception of Devaraj, the students responded clearly, 'An arranged marriage.'

In the blink of an eye, my students had forgotten all about Konomi, Aya, and Airin as they reverted to being loyal sons. It was heartwarming to see how deeply they had internalised what wider society considered common sense, how they didn't harbour even the slightest hint of disagreement or dissent.

'Love marriages often end in divorce,' Ganesha said. 'My uncle got divorced.'

He had to correct himself three times before he could get his sentence out clearly, but in other words, marriage oughtn't be a matter of personal will. In this country where caste, one's parents' professions, and even astrology are deeply intertwined, the choice between an arranged marriage and love isn't really a viable one.

However, there are still times when love wins out, when individuals encounter in another a spirit of mutual attraction. According to my students, it seemed that there were usually one or two elopements in every family.

Said Ananda, 'My cousin told my uncle he has a girlfriend.'

One day this cousin opened up to his father and told him that he had met a girl, now his girlfriend, at a temple. The father, until that moment listening on in stoic silence, removed his sandals and began to beat his son with them. Ananda told me with a carefree smile that his cousin had almost been knocked out cold before escaping to the police for protection. There was, it seemed, a deeper motive behind this thrashing – in the case of a love marriage, a dowry generally isn't required, which is often seen as a benefit from the perspective of the woman's family, while at the same time engendering intense resistance on the part of the man's.

However, all of this was predicated on the assumption that one had a family in the first place. Given that Devaraj had no relatives to whom he could turn in the event of an emergency, it was easy to imagine the difficulties and trouble involved being even more complicated than in a typical love marriage. And it was amid these hardships that Devaraj's dreams for the future took form as his own private kingdom of love, his own private image of love, as evoked by the following little story.

Once in the classroom I had the students practise writing some simple kanji characters. As I called them each up by name, they would approach the whiteboard and write the characters that I called out. Finally it was Devaraj's turn.

'Ear… Mouth… Eye…' I said in English, and Devaraj didn't hesitate to write the corresponding kanji characters one by one.

When I used a red marker to draw a circle, the Japanese equivalent to a tick, beside the character for eye, Devaraj suddenly said, 'Sensei. I saw a woman at the bus stop yesterday. She had very beautiful eyes.'

Not again, I thought, continuing to stare in silence at the textbook as Devaraj continued. 'I like beautiful women, so when I saw this very beautiful woman…' He paused there, leaning in and glancing upward. 'I saw her, and I wished she was my girlfriend. I want a girlfriend like her, I thought. And then I will have these eyes.'

He looked straight at me. Frankly, I didn't much like looking back at a man so handsome that it made the blood rush to my cheeks. But as much as I wanted to avert my gaze, the terrible light radiating from his eyes had already robbed me of all sense of free will. I could no longer turn away.

He raised his hand, pointed to those eyes of his, and asked, 'These eyes, what do you call them in Japanese?'

I don't know what exactly happened, but I must have blacked out for a brief moment, as the next thing that I knew, the textbook was flying out of my hands and I slumped down against the wall with both hands on the floor. A faint popping sound echoed near my ear, and when I ran my hand over it, I realised that the hair on both sides of my face was burned to a crisp.

Devaraj looked down at me, his smooth cheeks glistening in the fluorescent lights hanging from the ceiling. I could make out every last detail on his cheeks, my vision so unbelievably clear that I couldn't possibly be anywhere but hell. His mouth turned at the corners like a wash-and-wear shirt, and he said, 'What is the word in Japanese?'

'There is no word for it in Japanese.'

There could be no words to describe something that

didn't exist. No Japanese had eyes like that. Yes, the beginning of a heart-stirring love affair could always be found in the searing interplay between two pairs of eyes. The passionate world of Indian movies, filled with song and dance, was, I realised, entirely the result of just such a fateful convergence.

At that moment, I glanced up as a dull, heavy thud rang out and saw that two people flying overhead had collided over the Adyar far to my left.

A cloud of black and white feathers scattered in the bright morning sun. The black-winged flyer soon managed to somehow regain his bearing and flew away downstream at high speed, while the white-winged one made a large arc before tumbling into the murky river. It seemed that these aerial wings were equipped with GPS, and no sooner did the flyer crash into the water than an attendant rushed to the scene to quickly scoop up the cursing figure of the distinguished-looking executive with an oversized net. His seemed to be one of the latest models of aerial wings, complete with an automatic braking function, but that technology was still far from commonplace. Flying to work was supposed to be a privilege of the wealthy and those of high social standing, but lately, there seemed to be an increasing number of unauthorised flyers who operated beyond the purview of the law, many of whom had been tagged as violent in character. For countless mornings now, there had been frequent scenes of near misses if not outright collisions, so it was little wonder that so many individuals now flew while wearing imported woks on their heads for their own protection. This morning arena could be found only in India, where IT and worldly wonders were merged into one.

Like someone snapping awake upon realising that they are in a dream, like someone standing in a queue and forgetting what exactly they are waiting for, I found myself paralysed, unable to move amid the hustle and bustle – when all of a sudden I saw between the profile of a young man to my left and the smartphone that he was holding out in front of him the flowing surface of the ochre-coloured Adyar, and I wondered to myself if there really was a sea at the end of all this water.

Devaraj, unconcerned with all the goings-on around him, wore a puzzled look as he continued to plunge his rake deep into the hundred-year-old mud and pulled what he then unearthed to the sidewalk at my feet.

This time it was considerably smaller in size. After reaching down to retrieve it, I wiped the mud off an old coin imbued with a smoky hue. A thin chain hung from the rim, so it must have been a souvenir coin pendant.

'It's a commemorative coin, Sensei. From the Osaka World Fair.'

All at once, a voice rang out in my ear, and I raised my face. Beyond the wild commotion, I could see Devaraj pulling his rake, but I couldn't make out his expression from behind. Nonetheless, I knew intuitively that this was no mere voice, that it wasn't the result of vocal cords trembling deep in his throat. It was fuzzy and faint, like the mist on a river's surface after a rainy afternoon, and the content of its message quietly filled my heart.

This is what it said:

'When I was little, I once spent the better part of a year travelling by my father's side, roving from town to town in a small truck with a cage of young bears.

'For travelling showmen, certain times of year are more lucrative than others. Naturally, the off-season is during the monsoonal rains, which in South India are around October and November. However, those same months make up the dry season in the northern part of the country, so we sometimes embarked on long journeys. People tend to loosen their purse strings during major festivals, so those times are always the best to put on a show. In South India, the main events and the most profitable times of the year are Diwali, the light festival held in October or November each year depending on the Hindu calendar, and Pongal, the January harvest festival. In North India, Holi, the March spring festival, is one of the popular seasons, and we often journeyed northward around that time. I can't remember going to many large cities. It can be easy to secure large audiences in those kinds of places, but so many people want to watch without paying, and the cost of accommodation skyrockets. So my father mainly travelled to farming villages, and in farming villages, there are years of good harvests, and there are years of poor ones.

'If you go before the crops are harvested, people's purse strings tend to be tight, and you won't have much hope of doing business. As such, we usually spent the better part of the season in my home village, where my father would take on work from his local acquaintances, while

I would earn what I could by taking on errands such as babysitting at wealthy houses in the neighbourhood. I had been left in my village for a full year only once, back when the Kashmir conflict picked up steam. All three sons of a wealthy farmer had been serving in the military, leaving them unable to return, and so with no workers, the farmer asked to take me on. I mentioned before what else took place that year. My mother was working for a folk healer in the same village. She never accompanied my father on any of his travels.

'My mother and father were from the same village. My parents weren't allowed to marry, and so they eloped when my father was twenty and my mother eighteen. Maybe things are different now, but in the old days, it was normal for your parents to decide your marriage partner for you, and the mere act of falling in love was considered immoral.

'There have always been couples who choose to elope. Nonetheless, elopement is thought to bring immense shame to one's entire family, and those who do so are inevitably ostracised by their entire village, to the extent that people will look away if they spot them on the streets, relatives will refuse to speak to them, and everyone will exclude them from weddings and important village gatherings. It's seen as a matter of course that children should obey their parents, and parents who cannot command the obedience of their children are seen as the most unhappy of souls. Which is why, even today, you still hear about parents or siblings chasing after those who run off to marry someone out of love, all just to kill them.

Those involved in so-called honour killings are only rarely charged with any crime.

'The reason why my mother and father chose to elope was partly because the inhabitants of their village regarded one another practically as cousins, and for that reason, marriage between villagers had been disallowed for as long as anyone could remember. But that wasn't the only factor. On top of that, my father's parents refused to approve of the marriage on account of my mother having been abandoned as a child. People said that my mother's had been a difficult birth, that no sooner did she enter this world than her own mother cast her away, the midwife literally throwing her out the window when it was learned that she was a girl. That isn't an uncommon occurrence. Here in India, it's currently prohibited by law to determine the sex of a foetus by ultrasound because many parents will choose to abort if they learn that they're going to have a girl. Even when born, if the baby turns out to be a girl, she might find herself thrown into a canal or a garbage can, fed rat poison, or left somewhere in the house to starve to death without ever being breastfed. While sons can grow up to be breadwinners, daughters are not only unable to take care of their own parents in old age, they also need hefty dowries when the time comes for them to get married, and so are often unwanted. But I should turn back to the story at hand. Exhausted after giving birth, my mother's mother – my grandmother – awoke at dawn and stepped outside to do her business. By the window, she found some overripe fruit from the nearby papaya tree scattered all about, and amid that mess, she noticed something moving. Taking a few steps closer, she found the baby clinging to a papaya in the wan dawn light, licking the juice from the ruptured skin as though the fruit itself was the girl's mother. Seeing this, my grandmother took pity on the baby, carried her in her arms, brought her into the house, and managed to convince the family to raise her. According to the local custom, three months later, the family tattooed the baby's legs in the hope that she would grow up to be strong and free of disease, and that she would be reborn as a man in the next life. This would later lead to fatal complications, but no one could have known that at the time. There was one doctor of Western medicine in the village, but the cost of his services and prescription medicines was so high that most of the villagers turned instead to folk healers, who practised a trade that was half folk medicine and half witchcraft. My mother had worked as an assistant for such a folk healer ever since she was a girl. She never went to school, but she was a remarkably clever child. She only had to hear once about the types, effects, and formulations of traditional herbs that healers used in their daily treatments to remember them by heart. Apparently, she was responsible for chopping the herbs, drying them in the sun, roasting them, and doing all kinds of other work too, so the healer must have valued her skills. Even after eloping with my father, she continued to work for the folk healer, a woman called Hena, who was reluctant to let go of her given her deep knowledge of so many herbs and formulations. The villagers called Hena a witch behind her back, so she must have had a history of dubious practices. But at the same time, she was the most trusted of the several healers in the village, and people tended to go to her first when they found themselves suffering from some physical ailment.

'My mother told me that she had never accompanied my father on any of his tours, but she always made sure that he took a stock of medicine with him. As the Indian saying goes, *Pray, but first take your medicine.* Whenever I came down with a fever as a child, my mother's medicine would work wonders.

'In the autumn my father and I went north during Diwali to put on a show near Dharamshala. Before we got started, I walked around the village blowing a whistle to attract visitors, and it was then that I saw a woman peeping around an empty house. She quickly sped away when she noticed me, but I later saw her again under the Gandharva tree in the square, reading the fortunes of the villagers gathered there. Later, I realised that she must have been a spy, visiting the village under the guise of a fortune teller in order to gather information on its inhabitants, their households, and personal affairs. This was because that night, the village was attacked by more than a dozen bandits, with only the homes of wealthiest families being targeted.

'We had just completed a show in the village that day. It was festival season, the time of year when everyone has plenty of money to throw around, and as we had already toured several other villages, we had already earned ourselves a tidy sum. The inn where we were staying was also targeted by the bandits, and a man who looked like their leader threatened my father at knifepoint. "Hand it over," he demanded.

'"Spare us, please! With the fuel we have left, there's nowhere else we can go to do business. We're just traveling entertainers – if we go broke, we'll die in the street. You've already taken enough from the houses, haven't you? Turn us a blind eye, I beg of you."

'Yet despite my father's pleas, the bandit leader didn't bat so much as an eye. "You've heard the saying, eh? In this world, the only thieves who go uncaught are kings."

'To this my father had no response.

'"But it ain't just kings. You've got landowners, policemen, the military… Every which way you look in this country, it's just thieves, thieves, thieves. Sometimes I even pay 'em off myself. That's why I don't get caught. So why should I let you off the hook without paying up? Don't you go about telling me how to do my business."

'Behind the man, the fortune teller whom I had seen during the day stood near the entrance cradling a small girl in her arms, and it only took me a moment to notice that the child was unwell. Her cheeks and forehead were bright red, her breathing ragged. It hit me all at once, a selfless thought flashing through my mind.

'"Do you want the money or medicine for the kid?" I said to the bandit, who stared back at me in disbelief. "I have some medicine good for children's illnesses. I'll give it to you instead of the money."

'The fortune teller seemed to be the bandit leader's wife. The two of them consulted loudly for a minute, until finally the woman stepped toward me, holding out a hand to silence the bandit as she said, "We'll take the medicine." And so I gave her the remedy that my mother had prepared for me. The child's cheeks and forehead immediately blushed, and she fell sound asleep with a soft sigh.

'The bandit leader was overjoyed to see this, and with a bitter smile he said to me, "The other week, five people died in the next village over after taking potions from a fake doctor. The doctor died along with 'em though."

'Hearing this, I was amazed that he had trusted me. As the bandits left, leaving us and our earnings be, their leader said, "You've got my thanks. Here, take this. I've treasured it for years, but you saved my greatest treasure of all, so you can have it."

'The dull, turmeric-coloured coin pendant that he retrieved from his pocket was inscribed with words and symbols that I had never seen before.

'"It belonged to a Japanese man I found waiting at a bus stop in Dharamshala. He was fool enough to set his backpack down by his feet while trying to read a map. I found it in there."

'Apparently, the bandit knew that he was Japanese from his passport, also left in the backpack. There is a famous meditation hall in Dharamshala, and apparently the hordes of India-loving foreigners travelling back and forth from the city make for easy pickings.

'Anyway, the coin was no doubt Japanese. I could read the words *Expo'70* written in Roman letters, but the other characters must have been in Japanese script. I immediately fell in love with those symbols, feeling at home as my gaze passed over them, even if I didn't have any idea what they actually meant. I kept the coin close to my heart at all times. I never grew tired of looking at it whenever I had a free moment. I was always wondering what exactly those strange characters said, constantly imagining that they read this or that.

'The news came just as we were about to set off back to our home town. It gave no details, only saying that my mother had passed away. We went home, yet what we found waiting for us was enough to make us wish that we hadn't. My mother, I was told, had been arrested by the police, only to die during their interrogation. We later learned that she hadn't even been properly arrested or charged, only asked to accompany the police to answer some questions. But while there, she fell suddenly ill and breathed her last.

'It was Hena, the folk healer, who was arrested. A patient of hers, a pregnant woman, had died, and her husband complained to the police that the drugs prescribed by the healer were flagrant frauds. After the couple found out that they were pregnant, they went to Hena for a drug that would ensure that the baby was born a boy, as with their first child having turned out to be a girl, they were concerned about the prospect of having more daughters. Hena gave the pregnant woman detailed instructions for the formula: she was to take the medicine while deep in prayer, drink milk from a cow that had given birth to a bull within the last three months, avoid looking at the faces of other women in the household as much as possible, and hold an earnest wish in her heart for the child to be a son. Yet after five days of taking the medicine morning and night, the woman perished without any warning.

'My father must have known about my mother's condition. Shortly before she passed away, she would often lie down in the middle of the afternoon, even before finishing her usual housework, telling me only that she was tired. One time while we were out and about, we bumped into the only doctor of Western medicine in the village, who after no more than a quick glance, said to her, "You have jaundice, rather severe by the looks of it. You get tired easily, I assume? Does your body feel swollen? Do you have an upset stomach? Come to my clinic." The Western doctor seemed to be a friendly and well-regarded man, quite unlike how my mother and Hena had spoken about him. I didn't understand the precise meaning of all those words, but I knew that my mother was in poor condition, and that he was only trying to help.

'Much later, while at university, I had a chance to talk to a medical student who explained the likely cause and progression of the illness. He told me that my mother had most likely been in the late stages of hepatitis, that if it had progressed to cirrhosis, her blood vessels would have swollen into varicose veins, which if ruptured, could have led to haemorrhaging and death.

'"It was probably a tattoo that caused it," he told me. "You said she got a tattoo when she was born? That could have caused the initial viral infection." Indeed, it isn't uncommon in India for people to die prematurely because of tattoos that they receive as infants in the hope of long life. An acquaintance of the medical student seemed to have passed away from similar causes, though in his case the tattoo was meant just for fun, in imitation of an actor that he had seen in some movie.

'As if somehow having known that her time on this earth would one day come to a premature end, my mother had instructed my father that if she was to die, she wanted him to scatter her ashes in the Ganges River. Once her remains were swept away into the Ganga, all the sins from her infinite past lives would be washed clean.

'We had to hire a special car to transport her remains to Varanasi. Her body was wrapped in several layers of cloth, tied to a ladder-like coffin rack, and secured to the roof of the vehicle with metal fittings for transportation.

'Passing through a mountainous area on the journey there, we were stopped in our tracks by a rock fall, the aftermath of a landslide triggered by heavy rain. Left with no other option, we retraced our path more than a third of the way back up the mountain road, took a long detour, and finally arrived at Varanasi after three days and nights. It was the peak season, and the bathing ghats along the Ganga were crowded with pilgrims and foreign tourists.

'The fee that the driver charged us on our arrival was far in excess of what had been agreed when we set out from our home town. Yet the man was adamant. "It cost me three times as much as the planned course. Three times. Do you know how much the petrol alone cost me?"

'The firewood and funeral expenses amounted to another several thousand rupees, but we were already broke after paying the driver's additional fee.

'"I'll try talking to the cremators," my father said, heading off to request their services. As I waited at the ghat looking out over the Ganga, I found myself wondering whether my mother would have survived if only I had insisted on taking her straight to the clinic after running into the doctor in the village.

'An old lady waddled up from my right, slowly descending the steps of the ghat and stepping into the river still fully robed in her sari. Once she was waist-deep, she repeatedly scooped up handfuls of water with both hands and poured them over her head, her shoulders, her back, murmuring some invocation under her breath as she washed away her sins. Nearby, a young man squatted at the bottom of the stairs by the water's edge lathering his jeans and trunks with foam, while another man carrying a little girl in his arms was making his way down the stairs in an almighty hurry, stopping at the bottom to let the child relieve herself.

'After a while, my father returned. "I couldn't get any firewood," he said feebly. In short, he had been turned down at every corner. We were left with no choice but to let the river take my mother's body whole.

'My father crouched next to me in a crumpled heap. Hunched forward in resignation, he stared out over the waters of the Ganga. He didn't bring up the topic of my younger brother or sister who had been adopted out – partly, I suspect, in an effort to apologise for not coming home often enough on account of his constant traveling. His many infidelities had caused him no end of trouble in his relationship with my mother. But he forgave everything, and he was in turn forgiven, all thanks to the depths of love that existed between the two of them. I understood that better than anyone.

'He looked me square in the face. "You want to help cremate your mum, right?" he asked.

'When I nodded back to him, he pulled up close to me and lowered his voice. "There are foreign tourists all over the place here. They should have money on them, a lot of it. See him..." My father glanced over his shoulder, motioning with his chin to a traveller standing by a large tree with his luggage resting by his feet, wiping the sweat from his forehead as he perused a thick guidebook. "Go and grab that fool's bags. If he sees you, just start crying and tell him you're sorry, but you were hungry. You understand? There's no way he'll overreact with a cute little kid like you."

'I touched the pendant at my chest. What I had been asked to do was no different from the actions of that bandit – I was about to make someone else meet the same fate as the former owner of this coin. But I had to do it, for my mother.

'Varanasi, one of India's most famous pilgrimage sites, has some eighty-four ghats situated along a six kilometre stretch on the western bank of the Ganga, from Assi Ghat in the south to Adi Keshav Ghat in the north. In overall structure, the ghats are all similar, with temples, cafés, souvenir shops, and so forth rising up like steps from the riverside promenade to the west, followed by labyrinthine residential areas, and beyond those, marketplaces where all the local residents go to shop.

'My father and I were near Assi Ghat, where tourists sat in groups on the steps gazing at the Ganga. First, I climbed to the top of the stairs to avoid drawing attention to myself, then I scoured the place from above for potential prey. It didn't take long for me to spot a man in a green checked shirt reading a guidebook with his luggage unguarded by one side.

'I quietly descended the stairs from above and approached from behind. Just before I could reach his bag, a small, nimble hand snatched it from the other side. With a start, I watched on as a child of perhaps three or four, an agile little monkey, beat a quick escape.

'"Hey! What the…? Wait!" The traveller, catching on to the threatening presence, yelled out – and I, already nearby, leaped into motion to tackle the child, who suddenly bit down hard on my hand.

'"Ow!" I cried, releasing him. Nonetheless, I chased after him again, tracking him all the way to the nearby Tulsi Ghat where I caught him by the scruff of his neck. Snatching the bag from him, I shouted one of the few Hindi words that I knew, "Go!"

'By then, the monkey-like child was already fleeing up the stairs to my left. It wasn't long before I heard the ragged breathing of someone approaching from behind.

'"Ah, thank you! Thank you!"

'It was the traveller in the green checked shirt. I handed him the bag.

'"You're a lifesaver. Everything I have is in that bag. That could have been a disaster." The man looked to be middle-aged, maybe around forty years or so old. "Do you speak English?" he asked.

'"Yes," I answered.

'The man glanced down at the pendant dangling from my chest, his eyes widening in recognition. "Oh… Now that's a surprise," he murmured, taking the coin in his fingers. "*Expo '70*… A commemorative coin? From the Osaka World Fair? Is it real…? This is incredible…" He shook his head, then glanced up at my face. "Hey. Where in the world did you get this?"

'I fixed him with a smile. "It was a thank you for guiding a Japanese tourist," I answered.

'"Ah, I see… You know, I was there, the Osaka World Fair… I must have been around your age." The man's face was awash with emotion as he wiped the sweat from his cheeks.

'"Are you Japanese?" I asked.

'"That's right," he answered with a grin. "How old are you? You're pretty amazing for such a small guy. Your English is good too."

'I could hardly contain my excitement talking to a Japanese person for the first time in my life. "I'm five," I said. "I help look after the other local kids. I get paid for it. I go with them to the local school and sit by the wall of the school building. It's nice and cool there. There's an English classroom, and you can hear the teacher speaking in English through the window, so I repeat the sentences every day. I always memorise the new English words and sentences faster than the students in the classroom."

'"Huh… That's incredible alright…" The man, staring back with admiration, abruptly shifted his gaze behind me.

'Turning around, I spotted smoke rising high and black from the riverbank a few ghats up ahead. "It's the Harishchandra Ghat," I explained. "The smoke is from a funeral pyre."

'"A cremation?" the man asked. "You mean like at the Manikarnika Ghat? I've heard of that one."

'"There are two cremation ghats along the Ganga: the Manikarnika Ghat and the Harishchandra Ghat. The Manikarnika Ghat is bigger and more famous, and it's closer to the main ghats, so tourists usually go there."

'"Indian custom is to cremate the deceased and scatter their ashes in the Ganga, right? That's the usual way of mourning, isn't it?"

'Sensing that the man had taken a liking to me, I stood up straight and tried to answer him as solemnly as I could. "Yes. When cremated, the soul rises up to heaven with the smoke. Only the bones and ashes are released into the water, and the Ganga cleanses all their past sins."

'Then, before I could even think, my mouth was already moving entirely by itself. "Please. I want to hold a funeral for my mother."

'Frantically, I told him everything that had happened to bring me and my father here. "Without money, we'll have to release my mother's body straight into the river. But I want to give her a proper funeral, to cremate her. Even if it takes me the rest of my life, I'll pay you back, so please, please, lend me the money. Please."

'Deep in thought, the man looked straight at me for a moment before answering. "I won't lend you anything." Then, after a short pause, he added, "If I lend it to you,

you'll come to resent me. You know, I lost my own mother too… Around the same age as you, actually. Yes…" He pointed to the coin hanging around my neck. "It was the year of the Osaka World Fair. I went there with her, you know. She had been hospitalised for so long, so my father took us all there after she came home. That expo is my last memory of her. We didn't get to see the moon rocks, with the lines being so long, but my father bought me a commemorative coin too, you know. The same as that one. I took it hard when my mum died… It must be hard for you too, yes?"

'Overcome with emotion, the man paused there, staring across the Ganga. The wind coming in across the surface of the river buffeted his face for a moment, until finally he spoke up in a quiet voice. "When I saw that coin of yours," he said, pointing again at the pendant hanging around my neck, "I honestly couldn't believe my eyes… I keep it in a safe place, and every year, on the anniversary of my mother's death, I place it on the family altar. It's the exact same coin. It can't be a coincidence that I met you here. For my own mother's sake, I want to make sure you can mourn yours properly."

'Before I knew it, I was throwing myself in front of the man and pushing my forehead against the flat of his shoes in a gesture of respect. He seemed startled by this action, and when finally I rose back to my feet, he said, "There's just one thing… I want you to remember a Japanese word for me when you grow up… In Japan, this kind of memorial service is called a *kuyō*, an offering to the Buddha."

‘When I asked him what exactly the word meant, he replied, “To give a gift from the heart for the deceased. If you offer a *kuyō* to your mother, that memorial service will honour my own mother too. I'm sure of it.”

‘He asked me how much the funeral would cost, then silently handed me the money and left without sharing any means for me to contact or thank him.

‘I owe that Japanese man a great debt. It was thanks to him that my mother could go to heaven, that I wasn't forced to become a thief. If he hadn't offered me that money, I would have no doubt searched for another traveller's luggage to rob, and then I would have gone looking for another after that, and another, and another, until all that I ever did was seek out tourists to steal from.’

All of a sudden, I heard a screech of brakes like the hinges of a rusty barn door swinging open, and when I turned round, I watched as a yellow three-wheeled mini truck came to a stop on the bridge directly behind me.

An elderly woman in a sari handed the driver a folded bill and stepped down from the narrow interior of the vehicle, her braids adorned with layers of white jasmine bouncing vigorously on her plump back as she strode briskly out. No sooner did she reach the side of the road than she began digging with her plump hands through the mud.

When I turned back around, Devaraj had already disappeared. I was by now feeling rather intimidated to find myself teaching Japanese to someone capable of telling such a rich story of his own experiences, the kind of tale that you might find in the Tōyō Bunko's series of Asian literary classics. If the inhabitants of Suita in Osaka only knew that a commemorative coin from the 1970 World Fair, held in their own local neighbourhood, had become a prized treasure of an Indian bandit leader, they would no doubt be moved to tears.

Anyway, there was no end in sight to the crowds milling atop the bridge. The old woman's car was still stuck in the traffic jam, and the barrage of motorcycles, passenger cars, and three-wheelers arriving one after the other, all unable to push through the teeming throng, were backed up further than the eye could see. I was quite sure that all the people of Chennai, after watching these scenes on their television sets, would rush to this bridge within the next day or so, just as so many already were. Those who could afford to do so first approached the handrails to witness for themselves the ferocious power of the muddy water, which had risen several metres above its usual level and still now clawed violently at the bridge piers. Letting out gasps of surprise and satisfaction, savouring that pleasure, they set about inspecting the hundred-year-old mud for themselves. The more desperate among them didn't waste so much as a moment before crawling in and digging around in every direction. One wouldn't have expected their blind rummaging to turn up anything of interest, but surprisingly, that wasn't the case.

'I'm sorry, I'm sorry, I know I promised we would elope together to an acquaintance of mine in Andhra Pradesh… I'm so, so sorry…'

Pulling a man from the mud and wiping her thumbs across his face, calling out in a voice tinged with hints of sweetness, was the old woman who had just jumped down from the mini truck. Her face was drawn by long years of waiting, of harbouring in her heart a fire that could never be extinguished. Her white jasmine hair ornaments swung quickly on her sturdy shoulders.

The figure that she had dug out was that of a young man, perhaps around twenty years of age, who stared back vacantly at first, but soon seemed to recall the identity of the woman before him as he broke out in a cry and a laugh resplendent of the earthy scent of the hundred-year-old mud. 'It's okay, Irakkiyah. I know. Your mother was sick, and your younger brother and sisters...'

'I wanted to go with you, I really did. I wanted to go. I bought a new bag and a sari, and I packed everything and hid them in the attic. But I must have been found out, because that night, my father said to me, "I'm telling you, Irakkiyah, if you run off with that man, your mother and I will die. If you want to kill your own parents, go ahead and do it. Do you hear me, Elakkiya?"'

This sorrowful reunion was punctuated with the lively sounds of digging, of shovelling, of rummaging through and throwing to one side huge quantities of ancient mud in front and behind, left and right – and all the while voice upon voice sounded from every possible direction.

'That was fun, eh? Eh, Lokesh? Remember when we all went to Kashmir for the Ranji Trophy? It took three days to drive there, but it kept raining for a week, and the tournament was cancelled. It was the first time we had ever seen sleet, right?'

'During Diwali when I was five, I ate all the family sweets. You know, I was awful to you, Murugesh. Really, I blamed you for everything. Even though you came to work for us, your grades at school were always better than mine, and my mum was always nagging you. But it mustn't have been easy when you were let go like that, without any warning. You even stopped coming to school. I'm sorry for all of it, I really am.'

'I was the one who overheard you confess your heart to a friend, Mother-in-law. I was the one who spread those rumours about the neighbourhood. I knew your father's estate was close by, so I waited until the servants were about to head back to the village and made sure they overheard, all to turn it into a huge scandal. I've wanted to apologise for so very long.'

But even having borne witness to those fond reminiscences, those long-unburdened confessions, those heart-rending griefs, still I find myself unable to adequately explain the sight of an old woman, supported at one side by someone who must have been her daughter, shedding tears as she gripped the hands of a beautiful youth whom she had just dug out from the mud.

Letters unwritten, sights unseen, songs unheard, words unspoken, rain that had never fallen, lips forever unwetted – one and all, they each belonged to the mud of this past century. Lives that might have been, lives that never had been, postscripts left for later – all emerged from this great and expansive earthy mire.

With that I struck on a curious thought. In my language classes, I had been following the textbook without question, but in Japanese, we had so many words that all fell under the umbrella of the English term *life*, all of them different, all of them important. There was *jinsei*, the most common word used to refer to the notion of human life; *isshō*, the span of one's life through the ages; *inochi*, the idea of an innate life force; *seikatsu*, everyday life and living; and *ikimono*, living creatures and animals. At the time, I had thought those distinctions so tedious that I had let them pass unmentioned, but I would have to go back and explain the differences one by one. Indeed, the word *inochi* would appear in a conversation later in the textbook, and if I didn't introduce it properly beforehand, Devaraj would no doubt grill me over its proper usage. Feeling vaguely let down with myself, I stared out at the muddy lines stretching from one side of the bridge to the other, my mind growing numb as I took in the sight of so many people teeming within and without.

All these people who had been preserved in the mud of the past hundred years in their original forms – had they already, I wondered, faded from this world?

At that moment, a faint voice sounded softly from behind. 'I know how much you wanted to go to graduate school to study mechanical engineering, but you took a job at Hindu Technologies so you could marry me. Yet even then, my father still objected because of our different caste backgrounds…'

I turned my head when I heard the name of my company said aloud. It was a woman who had spoken, a beautiful and dignified lady in her fifties, embracing a handsome young man who looked to be in his mid-twenties. Given their appearance, the man could easily have been her son, but something about his face struck a chord in my memory. After ruminating for a long, quiet moment, I realised that apart from his age, he looked just like Vice President Karthikeyan, and so my curiosity piqued, I fixed the two in my gaze. I would never have taken Mr Karthikeyan, normally so serious and strait-laced, as a romantic, and so decided to file this moment away until it came time to negotiate a pay rise when my contract was up for renewal next year.

As I continued along the bridge, still packed to bursting with bodies pushing to and fro, a fierce argument erupted to my right.

'Hey, that's my nephew!'

'What are you talking about? He's been my best friend since middle school!'

'Quit joking around! He's my cousin! Take a look at this nose! He looks just like me, see?'

I watched on as a man in his mid-forties, pulled unawares from the mud by three pairs of hands and glancing around with a start, was thrown into the middle of a heated fracas. He too, I realised, looked vaguely familiar.

He had a ponytail, and his muddy face was covered in stubble, but I couldn't place him. Just as I was about to pass him by, I suddenly remembered – right, he was my fifth man. The one who had made me borrow from a loan shark, bought me a bowl of ramen noodles, and then promptly absconded. In a way, it was because of him that I too had washed up in this South Indian city. For more than ten seconds, I stared over my shoulder at his face, caked in muck, only to realise that the hatred I had once felt for him had already run dry.

With everything and anything covered in this endless mud, how could I know which memories were mine and which belonged to any one of the myriad others flocking around me? But those previous three who believed that they had unearthed their own memories from the mud had no such qualms, each of them squatting side by side in the mire as they stubbornly fought over what they each saw as their own.

Without warning, a woman reached out to grab my fifth man by the shoulder. 'Hey, hey, Sengodan? I had a lot of fun in Pondicherry drinking wine with those students. Where were they from again? The capital of Japan, right? So Hiroshima? No, wait, Nagasaki? I haven't had so much as a sip of wine since, ever since that prohibition order came into effect. I can't stand it! From Kerala to Bihar, everywhere you go, they're all now prohibition states! Hey, let's go to Pondicherry again. You can drink as much as you want there, right? We can take Pandian's car. His parents gave him a Suzuki, you know? And he hired a monk to pray for traffic safety…'

The woman was still talking when another figure beside her shook her hand roughly away, before slapping my fifth man – still at the centre of everyone's attention – on the back, turning him around, and then rolling the right sleeve of his T-shirt over his shoulder. 'Look here,

Sivakumar. You know what this is, right? It's that tattoo I got with you. We were so impressed with that movie we both had to get the same tattoo as the main actor. What do they call it, a panda? It's meant to be the strongest animal in the world, from deep in the mountains of Tibet. Look closely into those drooping eyes, see how ferocious it is? I want to be a man like that. You know, we used to go to the cinema every week. What was that actor's name again? Right, didn't he marry that Pakistani actress, the one who divorced that F3 racer who got messed up in an accident after driving too fast and ended up in hospital for drug addiction? Come on, let's see yours. And take Vaithiya with you when you…'

Once more, in the midst of this conversation, another face grabbed my fifth man by both shoulders, usurped his attention as he looked him square in the eye, and all but threw the tattooed figure headfirst into the mud. This robber, completely unconcerned, held the bracelet on his wrist, laced with fine turquoise stripes, in front of my fifth man's eyes and said, 'Hey, you remember this, Thyagarajan? The bracelet we pilfered from that stall in front of the Vishvanatha Temple back in high school? I didn't really want it, but I *did* want to get into a little mischief. So I called out, "Terrorist! A suicide bomber! Run!" The shopkeepers, the customers, everyone – they all went crazy. They flew into a panic and ran off without so much as glancing over their shoulders, and we made a clean escape. Remember?'

And so on and so forth, each new person tirelessly asserting their own memories of my fifth partner. He, at the centre of all this attention, remained unexpressive, no emotion or judgment passing across his face as he stared into the countenances that came and went before him. Indeed, it was impossible to tell if those blank, unresponsive eyes saw anything at all.

I wasn't sure whether or not it had anything to do with a past life, but a part of me still adored his weak smile, and as I watched these Indians compete for a nephew, a close friend, a cousin, I couldn't see him as anything other than a small-eyed middle-aged man of East Asian descent. I realised then that all these memories that had just come to mind – from a bottle of Yamazaki Twelve Years Old, to a mummified mermaid, to an unmistakable memento pulled from the accumulated mud of a century – were all now gone, and I could think of them only as someone else's, even if they had at one point all been mine. In fact, for as long as I could remember, probably ever since I lost my mother, I have had difficulty finding reality in the parts and pieces of this life that I call my own. It seems that our lives, no matter where we dig, are simply patchworks of countless other unspecified lives. And with that insight, I could think of myself only as something that had somehow managed to pull through a maze of obstacles. That I had had to come all the way to South India to fully grasp this left me feeling truly disappointed with myself.

Helplessly surrounded on all sides by the hustle and bustle of the crowd, I pushed on ahead in a state of helpless shock, while behind me an endless stream of Indians fought in a dead heat over my fifth man at the edge of the mud.

'Ah! Brother!' echoed a voice punctuating the commotion.

'Elavarasan! It's you, isn't it, Ilavarasan? How many years has it been?'

Two more figures, it seemed, had entered the fray.

The introductory Japanese class that I was in charge of was supposed to last four months, and while I had been looking forward to it finishing so much that I literally dreamed of seeing the end of it, it was clear that it would have to be extended indefinitely, at least until the flood was fully cleaned up. Most of the students had no doubt returned to their home towns, and there was no telling when they would be back in Chennai. I would simply have to wait for them to return before setting our sights on completing the textbook as a class.

All at once, as if to make a lie of the deep stagnation that had occupied the bridge up till now, the line of people, cars, and motorcycles ahead of me burst into motion, and Devaraj, keeping shoulder to shoulder with the figures around him, appeared before me once again. With his rake, he swept up the muddy whiskey bottle, the mummified mermaid and the commemorative coin from the Osaka World Fair, and with laboured breath, pushed them all under the handrail. The glass case must have broken into pieces in the mud, as he was forced to kick the tail of the mummified mermaid with one foot until it fell silently off the side of the bridge. His profile, as I watched, seemed to all but say, 'Yes, you're done. See you again in another hundred years.' As I stared at that familiar, wary countenance, that thin half smirk, I found myself letting out a deep sigh at the fact that I wasn't yet ready to sever ties with this young man and his propensity for telling tall tales.

He stopped his rake at the sound of a sharp whistle blaring from the far side of the bridge, before turning to me. 'Sensei,' he called out. 'How do you say *cancel* in Japanese?'

'*Torikeshimasu* – take back,' I answered.

'Before, I said women don't like children. I want to take that back.'

'Do you?'

'Sensei.'

'What is it?'

'Won't you go to the beach with me?'

'No,' I answered, almost losing my footing.

Before I knew it, I had reached the very end of the bridge. Leaping down the final step, my destination, the office, was there on my left.

www.ingramcontent.com/pod-product-compliance
Lightning Source LLC
LaVergne TN
LVHW051010080826
845145LV00009B/2549

* 9 7 8 0 6 4 8 9 0 1 1 9 8 *